# THE CURSE

# THE CURSE

## Emerald Trilogy:
## Book 2

### QUINN MINNICH
*Anya Minnich*

Quinn Minnich

# Contents

# I

# Storm Clouds Gather

There was once a great land called Tarenthia, which was surrounded on all sides by the Great Sea. But Tarenthia was not the only country to be found in those waters, for many other lands and islands existed as well—some big and some small, some near and some far. The closest of these countries, however, was a place known as the Shadowlands.

The Shadowlands measured half of Tarenthia's size and lay not very far away. It was to the west, and with a good ship one could sail there within one to three days, depending on the port of departure and whether the winds were favorable. Now the Shadowlands was nearly cut in half by a great river that ran east to west. North of that river was a great fortress, and beneath that fortress was a great dungeon. Within that dungeon was a large cell, and within that cell there slept a young dragon. The dragon's name was Ember, and he was dreaming...

*Ember prowled the dominion of his mind, basking in the joy and power that came with freedom. All around him, the surroundings took no distinct shape—for dreams care not about unnecessary details—but bore the impression of many places at once. The mist shrouded jungles and deserts, forests and plains and seas; it took on the feel of them all, but formed none in detail. Anywhere there was freedom, Ember seemed to be. He ruled over all; there were no boundaries or dangers—just an unending domain where he was unconquered, independent, proud, fearless, and free.*

*It began to go wrong when the other dragon appeared. Ember saw him off in the distance with scales the exact shade of emerald-green as his own, and as Ember drew closer, the dragon began to mirror other features. In fact, the nearer Ember got, the more like himself the other dragon appeared. At last, he stood no more than ten yards away and saw that the other dragon was indeed an exact replica of himself, though half his size.*

*Ember snorted, but the other dragon did not take notice. He stared to the left into the distance, as if waiting for someone. Ember turned to look and saw a man coming toward them, a man that instantly filled him with dread and anger—a man whose very presence seemed to contaminate his whole world of joy. It was a man he knew well.*

*Peace.*

*The smaller dragon was waiting for this man, waiting calmly and with contentment—though a sad kind of contentment. As the man continued to come closer to the smaller dragon, Ember growled angrily.*

*"Get away from that man!" he snarled. "Get away from him!"*

*The other dragon turned his head slowly to look at him, his eyes sad like those of a prisoner. "Please, give me this once. Let me have just a moment when I can feel his touch again."*

*"No! Leave him!" cried Ember, and as the man still approached and the phantom version of himself turned to greet him, Ember roared and charged. His horns sank deep into the smaller dragon's side, through the wing and knocked him off his feet with tremendous force.*

*Ember lifted his head and roared at him, but the dragon only turned to look back toward the image of Peace. For a brief moment the figure stopped and seemed to waver in the air like smoke. Then it faded away and disappeared.*

*The smaller dragon's head slumped toward the ground, and a tear trickled from his eye.*

*"Why?" he begged. "Why did you have to do that? It's so rare that I see him anymore. I'm destined to never meet him in life again; why do you deprive us of meeting, even in dreams?"*

*"You," growled Ember angrily, "You are supposed to be dead! The Curse killed you. Why are you here?"*

*"I've always been here," said the other dragon. He made an attempt to get up, but then gasped in pain and fell back down, breathing heavily. "You can shut me up...crush me into the farthest corner of your mind...but there will always be a part of you that remembers—that remembers what it was like to have peace."*

*"I have peace!" roared Ember. "I'm not dependent on that man for it any longer; why do you insist on poisoning my life with memories of the past?"*

*The other dragon laughed weakly. "Peace? You know nothing of peace. Joy and elation and power and greed you may have, but you have forgotten what it was like to have calm content, to be loved."*

*"You will die!" cried Ember rising up on his hind legs. "Die! Be gone! Never come to me again!" And he fell upon the helpless dragon, blasting it with fire and tearing into its chest with his claws...*

With a start Ember awoke, breathing hard. It was difficult to see

in the dungeon, but he felt the cold damp stone and steadied himself. Desperately he called out to Deception, longing for comfort.

In only a few moments there was the jingling of keys, the creak of an iron gate swinging open, and then the footsteps of a man. Ember stood as Deception rounded the corner. His face was concerned.

"What is the matter, my Ember? I heard you and felt that you were greatly distressed. Did you have a bad dream?"

*Yes,* Ember said to him, knowing the man's Link would detect his thoughts. *I don't understand it. He was there, and I was afraid.*

Deception walked up and held out his hand. Ember touched it with his muzzle and felt immediate relief. Joy flooded him and seemed to wash away the disturbance of his dream. He closed his eyes and basked in the excitement and hunger it created. It was pleasurable, but not really serenity and peace. The words of the smaller dragon wormed their way back into his mind.

"You saw yourself?" asked Deception. Through his Link, he had been able to gather glimpses of Ember's memories.

*Yes. I saw myself wanting my old Rider. Why? I thought you had a spell that would free me from my old state of mind.*

"Yes, I do, and it is working. But you have to give it time. That part of you is but a fading memory, it will disappear soon, and you will be entirely free. Did you kill him?"

*Yes, I did.*

"Then he will bother you no more."

*He said that I had forgotten what peace was. That I can't feel contentment.*

"He lies," said Deception. "And besides, what is peace? It's being content with something less; it's falling short of your true potential. You should always be rising higher, finding more levels of elation. That is why hunger is better than love. It is unending, inexhaustible. It always promises something more."

Ember nodded slightly and hummed, desire and excitement rushing through him.

"Now Ember, you don't mind being kept in the dungeon, do you?"

Ember shook his head. *No; it matters not to me where I am.*

"Even if you were beaten and whipped? You still would not mind?"

*No. What you give me is all I want; I do not care what else happens to me.*

"Good. Then I will leave you here for now. Remember, you are safe from being taken. The Curse will keep that man from imprisoning your mind again. Just trust me." He lifted his hand and began to walk to the prison doors.

*I will trust you; do not worry. But all the same, I would prefer if you could get rid of the man entirely. Then I am sure he will leave my dreams.*

"Oh, we will," said Deception soothingly. "Soon, that man will die. But we have no need to chase after him; he is coming to us. I will make all the arrangements. No need for you to worry."

Ember nodded. *Thank you, my master.*

Deception smiled. "Sweet dreams, my Ember."

* * *

Out on the Great Sea, somewhere between the distant shores of Tarenthia and the Shadowlands, there sailed a royal vessel. Up in the crow's nest the lookout squinted toward the setting sun as he had done all evening and all the afternoon before. He thought he saw something and looked again. This time he was sure of it: the dark silhouette against the brightness in the distance. He looked down and spotted a sailor working on the rigging halfway down the mast.

"Land ho!" he called out. The sailor looked up and saw the lookout pointing. "Land ho," he called again.

"Aye," the sailor replied, nodding, and then looked down to see a man at the base of the mast with a mop and a bucket of sea water. "Land's been spotted!" he hollered. The man looked up and his eyes widened. Immediately he dropped his mop and ran across the deck to where the captain stood at the wheel consulting with the navigator.

"Captain!" he called out with a salute. "Captain! Land's been spotted."

"Aye; return to your post," barked the captain, and the man returned to his mop. Leaving his navigator at the wheel, the captain turned and stepped solemnly across the deck to the ship's main cabin. He stopped briefly at the door and considered knocking, but when he found it slightly ajar, he decided against any delay and entered.

Inside there was a large bed, lining the walls were shelves of books, and upon the floor was a desk covered in charts and papers and letters. A man stood in front of the bed with his back to the door. His right hand

was visibly scorched and hung by his side; his left hand held a sword, the hilt likewise blackened.

The captain cleared his throat. "Peace, the Shadowlands have been sighted."

The man turned, the sword he held still clutched tightly in his hand.

"Finally," he said.

"It was just spotted by the lookout, so I would say that given his visibility and our current favorable wind, we should be no more than half a day's journey out."

"Good. Make way for it with full sail and have the men prepare to head ashore as soon as possible."

"Yes, my prince, I will. But before I go, I wondered if I could speak with you alone."

"Certainly," said Peace.

The captain closed the door and came to sit on the bed. Peace did likewise on the other side, still clutching his sword. The captain looked at it and sighed. Ever since the battle on the shores of World's End, Peace had been practicing and sparing with his left hand. He had grown fairly good too, having bested several men during the voyage. He could still move his right hand, but not like he once could and not without pain. The captain looked up from the sword and into Peace's eyes.

"Peace," he said. "I speak to you not as the commander of this ship, but as your friend. You need not do as I say, but I ask that you listen to my advice."

Peace nodded. "Of course."

The captain took a deep breath. "I don't think that you should go through with this. We are still a ways out and there is no shame in turning back."

Peace shook his head. "I'm sorry; I cannot do that."

"I know that you have lost your dragon," said the captain, "but if we went back home you could be given another, and you would once again be permitted to take the throne. Custom states that the Dragon Rider must have his dragon when he is given the crown, but there is nothing stating that it must be his original dragon. Things like this have happened before, to Riders of old who lost dragons in battle."

"No," said Peace gently but firmly. "I could never do that. I would be unable to give my new dragon the love and care it deserved, and in our travels I could never cherish it as I did Ember. It wouldn't be right for him, for either of us, as long as he still lives."

"But what about the good of the country?" asked the captain. "What about Highland and Tarenthia? What will happen to us all if we lose our next king?"

"I made an oath that my actions were to be done first for the good of my dragon and then for the good of Tarenthia."

The captain sighed. "I know how much you loved him; but even if we are successful, things can never be the same as before. I don't think we can reclaim what was your childhood companion."

"It's more than that!" Peace said angrily. "Yes, I loved him and, yes, I would want things back the way they were, but this isn't about me. If I knew that Ember was in a better place, I could learn to deal with it; but he's not. He's in the hands of a mad man who will destroy him and use him to kill others as well! If he were dead, I would be more at ease, but this is imprisonment, this is sickness! I can't leave him like this, even if saving him will cost me my life."

The captain sighed compassionately. "Peace, I want to redeem Ember just as much as you do, and I would gladly die a thousand deaths just to see the two of you reunited as you should be. "But," he almost choked on the words, "but is this the best way? You know that I and everyone else on this ship would gladly give our lives at your command, but we number only one hundred fifty and two griffins. And we are sailing to the Shadowlands, a land which we know nothing about, and from which few have returned alive."

"One of them was my father."

"Yes, he did—he and Glory made it back. But none of us have; we know nothing of what we are getting into, and this is Deception's own country. If he outwitted you in Tarenthia, think of what he will do here with armies and kingdoms at his command. And if he does have dragons as he says, others besides Ember, then how can we hope to possibly stand against him?"

"Because we are fighting on his own soil, and he will be overconfident. Pride will be his downfall. He will want to be there when we are taken and so he'll likely bring Ember. All I need is one moment with Ember and everything will be right. We do not need to overcome Deception's armies."

"But what of before? You failed to reclaim Ember on the shores of World's End!"

"But I almost did! For just a moment I felt him coming back to me."

The captain stood, but his eyes were sad. "Then I hope for your sake that you will be given another chance." He put his hand on the door, but then stopped and turned. "I do suggest, however, that we prepare a more detailed plan. Some of the men are nervous. They will fight better if they are given a stronger hope, or if they know we stand a better chance."

Peace rose as well. "I would have gladly brought the whole army of Highland with me if I could; but this was all the King could spare."

"It isn't necessarily an army the soldiers want. Sometimes a renowned fighter or a skilled general can take the place of many men."

Peace looked at him sternly. "What are you trying to say?"

"Why?" asked the captain. "Why did we not bring Justice?"

"Justice?" said Peace with a scowl. He turned away. "Do not speak to me of my brother."

* * *

Back across the sea, on the western cliffs of Tarenthia, there stood the kingdom of Highland. Named for the high plains upon which it was built, the city was the largest and the mightiest in the entire land, perhaps in all the world. Its walls were tall and stately, its people well-housed, and its streets widely paved. Each ring of defense stood higher and thicker than the one before it, and within the strongest walls, on the very edge of the cliffs overlooking the sea, stood the King's castle. It was tall and magnificent, big enough to house all the people of Highland if need arose, and stocked with provisions to last years if a siege should befall it.

In the center of the castle, high above the many floors and chambers, was the great throne room that looked out through tall windows across the entire expanse of the kingdom. But the throne room was not the highest point, for from the corners of the castle rose four great towers stretching to spear the clouds above.

In the southwest tower, the one affording the clearest view of the sea, was a well-built young man. He paced the floor restlessly, a katana strapped to his left side and a dagger to his right. Every once in a while, he would stop to stare out the window and mumble angry words.

By and by, there were footfalls on the tower steps below and then the creaking of hinges as the door was opened. A man wearing royal robes and the king's crown emerged carefully from the opening.

"Ah, Justice; I thought I would find you here."

Justice did not turn to look at his father. He stared out at the open sea toward the sunset as he spoke. "Why did you let him go?"

The King sighed. "It was in his heart to leave. I could not stop him."

"He will die out there. You know that he cannot succeed."

The King looked down and shook his head slowly. "Yes, I know that he will fail."

Justice spun around. "Then why? Why did you allow him to go? His mission is both pointless and impossible. Even if he does find Ember, that dragon should be tried for treason and put to death. What can Peace hope to gain?"

"Peace hopes to save that which he loves most. It is who he is, to love dragons."

Justice snorted. "Why couldn't he have loved something more natural? Like a woman, or a kingdom, or his people? Instead, he chases after beasts." He grunted and turned back toward the window. "Sometimes I wonder how the two of us can even be brothers."

"You have more in common than you realize," said the King, softly closing the door. "What's more important, the two of you complement each other, providing what the other needs. It is very hard to have peace without justice." The King turned away and his face darkened slightly. "But it can be very easy to have justice without peace."

Justice turned. "Why do you say that?"

The King looked back to him. "Tell me, my son. Have you ever wondered why I chose Peace to be the Dragon Rider and not you?"

"I have wondered, but I have trusted your decision."

The King turned toward the window. "You would have been the natural first choice. You were the eldest, and I saw that you would act fairly and never use your power for personal gain or outside of the law. You excelled in every trait a king should have, except for one."

"Which was that?" asked Justice.

"You never learned to love."

"Love is a weakness. It gives your enemies power over you, and it impedes objective judgment."

"And yet it was what you needed most of all. Love was the one thing Peace did have—although he was deficient in nearly every other aspect. Of course, that was no surprise. No one is born worthy of becoming king. We all have propensities for good, but also for bad; we must be taught whatever it is we are lacking."

"Then did you think that Peace would be easier to teach than I?"

"In a way. You see, our method of training the next king is through the Dragon Rider Pact. Certainly it keeps the nations at peace, but that is only a side effect. Its real purpose is to get a man and a dragon to balance each other out, to learn from each other so that they can take the throne together as a unit."

The King walked across the floor and looked through another window. "All dragons are by nature more prone to aggression and bravery. I saw that pairing you with one would only heighten your sense of justice. Certainly you would only lead your dragon to do what was right by the law, but nearly all of Tarenthia would be destroyed because of it."

"Why?" asked Justice. "What is wrong with enforcing the law? I thought that our traditions were good and righteous."

"They are," said the King, "but they can only convict. All of us break the law at one time or another. All of us err. I never would have become King if I had received the full punishment for all of my mistakes. It was mercy that made me who I am, and it is mercy that I show. A dragon never could have taught you that.

"Peace on the other hand, was deficient in exactly the opposite respect. He was too merciful, too loving, too willing to forgive. I saw that a dragon would be the perfect thing for him; he would learn when to follow through with wrath, and his dragon would learn when to hold back. That is why Peace was made the Dragon Rider; not because you could not be taught, but because you could not be taught in that way." The King stared out over his kingdom and sighed. "Together, their rule would have been legendary."

"But it was a disagreement that separated them," countered Justice.

"That disagreement should never have taken place—at least, not to the degree that it did. Deception aggravated events to separate a friendship that in a few years' time would have grown too strong to break." The King sighed again; this time heavier. "And that is why Peace will fail. He

lacks the hardness and the strength that Ember gave him. He does not know how to combine love and justice." The King turned to look at his son. "That is why he will fail; but that is also why I had to let him go."

Justice rested his elbows on the windowsill and grunted. "Still, he should not have gone. Not only will he fail, but he was needed here."

Justice looked out over the kingdom and his father next to him did likewise. Stretching out before them lay the great expanse of Highland, majestic and peaceful. But beyond the outermost walls there was camped an army so great and so vast that its numbers stretched out across the plains into the distance. Among the tents there waved the banners of six different kingdoms, and over them flew nine dragons—all larger than Ember and all equipped with riders, ready for war.

Justice grunted angrily. "Peace could have stopped them. The kingdoms fear me, but they respect him. He could have prevented this; he always had that touch for diplomacy. But now when we need him most, he is gone." He looked out over the vast expanse of the enemy facing them. "I had hoped that Highland might endure forever," he said.

The King chuckled. "No nation ruled by man can do that. We are too depraved and corrupted to rule righteously for eternity. Perhaps it

is better this way. Is it not nobler for us to fall in battle, fighting for truth, than to be brought down from within, years later, by a line of selfish kings?"

"But we will still fight?" asked Justice.

"Yes, of course we will fight," said the King quickly; but then he turned back to look out the window toward his kingdom. His face was sad. "But even if we won, it would still mean nothing if Peace were lost."

# 2

# Oceans Rise

Ruthless was a hardened war general whose years of experience had made him cold, cunning, and cruel. Now, as he marched up the flight of stone steps, he muttered to himself, thinking about the news he bore. He came to the top and entered the throne room. A man stood in the center, reading over a list inscribed on parchment. Ruthless knew that it contained news of five new dragons which had been found up north and integrated into the army. He knew that his own report, however, would be of greater importance.

"Deception, he is here."

Deception turned around as he looked up from the parchment. He smiled, "So, he finally made it."

"Aye. I have received word that he landed yesterday evening with a force between one and two hundred."

"And did your patrol at the shore do as I instructed?"

"Yes. I have received word that they roughed them up quite a bit. But my men did not seek to kill."

"Good. So how does Highland's force stand?"

"A little over half injured."

"Even better. Perhaps that gave Peace a taste of what he is dealing with. Where is he now?"

"He and his men seek sanctuary in a city called Hope, about half a mile inland."

"Did he not leave? He chose to stay?"

"That is correct."

Deception was silent for a moment. Then quietly he asked, "Hope shelters them?"

"So my sources say."

"That town has always been a thorn in my side; they've resisted assimilation, built themselves a city as close to the sea as they could...." He was silent for a moment longer, but Ruthless could see a smile creeping across his face. "Prepare Ember," he said at last. "Peace no doubt misses his dragon; I think it's time we gave him a proper welcome."

* * *


Peace listened quietly as he was shown around the city of Hope. It was a small, compact town with a single outer wall encircling it. Within the wall, houses, stables, and markets were placed throughout in, more or less, an orderly manner. There was no palace, nor division between the rich and the poor, for the whole kingdom was governed by the people, all having a common goal in mind. The only other distinctive aspect of the city was a single stone tower constructed right in the center, rising up two to three times the height of the wall. It was open at the top; Peace eyed it with curiosity.

"What do you use the tower for?" he asked Defiance, one of the civil leaders who had offered to show him around.

"That?" he asked, looking up at it. "It serves several purposes. One is to watch the sea and spot any ships that might sail here. Additionally, it serves to watch for invading armies. There is also a skylance at the top—though thankfully we have never needed to use it."

Peace grunted. "A skylance? Against what threat? Not griffins I suppose."

"Oh no, griffins are very rare here. Many of our citizens were quite surprised to see yours." Defiance turned his head to look at the large, makeshift shelter where the two injured beasts were being held. Both had been severely wounded in the attack that had followed the landing.

"Then the skylances are meant for killing dragons," Peace said coldly.

"Well, yes, they are. Dragons are wilder and more populous here than in your country. They were always unstoppable until Deception brought a secret from Highland that could tame their newborn hatchlings. We know that he has dragons at his command now, and so we have the skylance as a precaution. We also have several more stored away in the base of the tower."

"I want them destroyed," said Peace angrily. "They won't serve you any real protection anyway; I know well that dragons can dodge the bolts...although not always."

"Why do you say that? Was your dragon once hit?"

"Yes," said Peace quietly. "Once, during the first year of our Sending Out, we had to break into a small castle that refused to reason with us. As we were flying in, a hidden skylance fired upon us and the arrow impaled Ember through the base of his wing. I can still hear the cry of pain it drew from him. We defeated the king, but afterward Ember could barely stand and was unable to fly for over a week." Peace looked away sadly as he recalled the story. "Had the arrow struck at a slightly different angle, it would've pierced his heart through the gap between the scales at his wing. I very nearly lost my companion that day."

Defiance placed a hand on Peace's shoulder. "I understand. The skylances will certainly not be used while you are here. It is not our mission to bring down dragons anyway." Defiance smiled. "I hope to finally see a dragon within our walls that is a friend and not an enemy. I look forward to reclaiming yours with you."

Peace smiled and continued walking. After a few minutes he said, "I'm glad we found you. You are a valuable ally, and I am thankful that you offered us protection after we were attacked on the shore."

"I am glad we were here too," said Defiance with a sad smile. "I fear that no other town is likely to offer you help. You are lucky to have landed here and not somewhere else."

"Really? There are no other nations in the Shadowlands that would ally themselves with Highland?"

Defiance shook his head sadly. "I'm afraid not. For many years the people in the Shadowlands were ruled by greedy kings that fought and squabbled with each other. But when Deception appeared he united nearly all nations together with his smooth words, into one great military force commanded entirely by himself."

Defiance smiled again. "Except the people here...we had heard stories of a distant land, where a kingdom named Highland ruled its people with fairness and justice. From many different cities and nations we came, united by the vision to leave our oppressed lives and seek something better. We came here, and those with greater faith sailed east, hoping to find your fabled land. The rest of us, however, who were not ready to leave our own country, settled here next to the sea in hope that one day a ship from Tarenthia might be spotted, and that all would finally be put right."

Defiance turned to face Peace. "For years now we have defied Deception's orders and held our post, hoping that you might come. Now that you have, we welcome you. But I fear the danger we are all in. Before, Deception never bothered us because we were small and insignificant to him. Now that you are here, however, I feel that we will finally be attacked. We will defend you with our lives, but I do not know how well this city will hold."

Peace nodded. "If I can get Ember back, I am sure that you will be saved. Let us hope that Deception brings him to us ahead of his forces."

"Aye," said Defiance, "let us hope that he does."

* * *

Justice's battle to save Highland was nearly over—and he had lost. Everyday Justice had led the armies out in full force against the invaders and fought ruthlessly for every gate. But there was no way to counter the dragons. Despite being known as the nation that trained them, Highland was surprisingly unprepared to combat the winged, fire-breathing beasts.

The city had always been a sanctuary for dragons and so there were no skylances. With the Dragon Rider gone, the only remaining dragon in the nation was Glory, the King's dragon who, while much larger and more powerful than the invading dragons, was gaining in years. The King had refused to take her out, and Justice could see why: as long as there was hope, his people would continue fighting for Highland, but if they should see their King fall in battle, then all would be lost. Even so, Justice grew angrier and more desperate each day as the invaders took more of the city.

"I don't see why you won't send out the griffins," muttered Justice one day to the King. "They are the best defense against the dragons we have."

The King shook his head. "You know that they would be slaughtered. Even if we had a hundred, they would still be torn apart."

"But at least they could hold them back," stormed Justice. "I understand why you do not fight, and I do not blame you for it; I also understand why you have chosen me to lead our men. But I can't defend us as long as you interfere with my methods! You shelter our griffins and the dragons rain fire upon us; we try to fight against their men, and you order us to retreat!"

"The way you are fighting, our soldiers will die," said the King firmly. "They will be slaughtered if you try and hold back the invasion."

"We can't hope to win this war unless we make a stand!"

"I am trying to protect my subjects."

"And so am I! But as each day passes, we lose more and more of the kingdom! We cannot retreat forever; what will be your plan when there is nowhere left to run?"

"I will fight them myself," said the King gravely.

"But the men need you!" Justice chafed, pacing restlessly. Then he looked up. "Maybe you could let me ride Glory. Perhaps then I could combat the dragons and hold our defenses. Then even if the worst happened, you would still be here to lead the men."

The King shook his head. "I cannot allow that."

"Why? What other option do we have?"

"For one it's tactically unwise, as you have no experience riding a dragon. But more importantly, I cannot allow it because I love Glory with all my heart. In her, I see reflected my people, my kingdom, and even my own sons. I have spent over thirty years by her side and if we are to die, then we will do so together."

Justice nodded and turned away. "I thought so; Peace said something similar once."

The King sighed. "Justice my son, if you are to ever understand the Dragon Rider Pact, then you must learn that dragons are our companions, not our tools. We protect them even as much as they protect us; they cannot be sacrificed for the greater good."

And so Justice was forced to fight all his battles on foot. Without the presence of his father, and without any other form of airborne defense, Justice had no choice but to continue retreating. He fought ruthlessly, he used every trick he knew, but in his heart he knew that it was all pointless. No matter how hard he and his men fought to hold each gate, the dragons could always fly in from above and decimate their forces.

One by one, the enemy took each ring of defense, forcing the citizens to flee closer and closer to the castle, until finally that was all there was left. Now, with the invading kingdoms assembled in formation outside the castle gates for the night, and with nine dragons circling the air above, Justice made one last climb to the southwest tower to look out over the dark, glistening sea.

"My brother," he whispered, "may your fortune prove to be greater than ours."

* * *

When night fell, Defiance's prediction was proved accurate. It was the time of the new moon, and only the light of distant stars pierced the darkness blanketed skies. Peace was walking along the inside of the wall when the horn came, a steady long blast that seemed to cry out in sadness and mourning. Peace quickly found his way by torchlight up to the battlements and looked out over the wall.

The invading army would have been impossible to see in the dark had it not been for the lanterns and torches they carried. There appeared to be around five hundred of them, all on horseback, and all riding furiously with great shouting and hollering, apparently preferring speed over stealth.

Peace raced down the ramparts to the ground and found Defiance already calling out orders to his men. "Do not let them through! Hold the gate at all costs. All archers—to the wall immediately—give them a taste of who we are! Swordsmen—station yourselves behind the gate!" He stopped shouting as men ran all about him. Peace took the moment to speak with his new friend.

"What are our chances?" he asked. Defiance turned to look at him; his face was fierce and determined.

"Our chances are good," he said, "if we can hold the gate. They are a relatively small force, so if we can keep them outside our walls and rain arrows upon them, we should be able to hold. Thankfully, there appear to be only the horsemen."

There was suddenly a great commotion at the east gate and Defiance ran to it. "Men, to me!" he called out. "Stab spears through the gate. Archers, fire down upon them. Hold them back!"

Peace backed up as soldiers all around rushed to follow orders, and he left Defiance to organize the defenses. Turning, he shouted orders to his own men, "Swordsmen and archers well enough to fight—head for the gate and follow Defiance's commands! We must not lose this city! Protect the griffins! I don't want them wounded further."

Around him, men scrambled to obey, and Peace watched with relief as more and more soldiers gathered around the gatehouse. Perhaps they would win. Maybe they would hold back the attacking wave.

Just then, the great horn atop the tower sounded again. Peace listened as it bellowed once, then twice, then a third time. He ran to Defiance and found him staring blankly ahead, his eyes wide.

"What's wrong?" asked Peace desperately. "What does the horn mean?"

Defiance tuned slowly to him, his voice trembling. "It's the system we use; the horn is to blow once if there is danger by land, twice if danger by sea..." He looked slowly upward, "...and three times if by air." Peace looked up with him into the darkness.

"Dragons? But how could the lookout even tell? It's so dark."

"The lookout is well trained," said Defiance turning back toward his men. "He saw their silhouettes blotting out the stars."

Suddenly, the wall behind them exploded in fire. Peace whirled around and saw a glimpse by the light of the flame of the fleeing dragon above. Fire exploded again on another portion of the wall and then a third time on a nearby building.

All around, ranks of men melted into confusion as soldiers began dropping their weapons and running to avoid the fire that fell from the sky. Peace leapt away from the wall as it lit up in flames before him. Over the chaos he could barely hear Defiance's voice calling out, "Stay together men! Hold your ground!"

Peace ran to an open area and looked about him in disbelief. Blazes flashed all around. It was nearly impossible to see the dragons above except for the brief moments when a blast of flame would provide illumination. He counted five dragons, possibly as many as seven, although there certainly could have been more; all of them seemed to have riders, who shouted and directed their great mounts. Though Peace strained to see, all the dragons he caught glimpses of seemed far too big to be Ember.

There was suddenly a great commotion and the sound of many cries behind him. Peace spun around and watched with horror as the battlements above the gatehouse were bathed in flame by two passing dragons. The archers were running and shouting, pushing each other, and hurling their flaming bodies off the wall. Peace realized suddenly that he no longer heard Defiance's voice and wondered when he had ceased calling out. The scene was utter chaos with soldiers running all over, injured and aflame.

Desperately, Peace tried to gain control. "Hold together!" he shouted. "Do not lose hope!"

A commotion caught his eye and Peace turned back to see a dragon, slightly smaller than the rest, land with great force in front of the gate and scatter the soldiers guarding it. Flames reflected dully off its deep blue scales as seven men leapt down from atop the beast and fought their way into the gatehouse.

"No!" cried Peace, rushing toward them with sword drawn.

The dragon was roaring, blasting brave soldiers with fire, and scaring away the rest. Peace ran even more desperately toward the beast that guarded the gatehouse, not thinking of his own safety. In the back of his mind, he wondered if perhaps the dragon had been given orders not to kill him, but he didn't have time to seriously consider that possibility. At the moment the dragon was distracted by two fleeing swordsmen.

But as Peace ran closer, the beast turned to look at him and its mouth opened to shoot fire. Suddenly, an idea struck him; with a cry Peace dropped his sword, leapt forth, and placed his hand on the creature's forehead.

Peace had never removed his Link, and so, of course, he had been able to gather glimpses of the dragon's thoughts. But with the physical connection came a torrent of feelings and thoughts and longings that ran throughout the creature's mind. Peace felt anger and fear and turmoil, but upon deeper probing he sensed a ravenous hunger—hunger for something unknown, similar to the hunger he had once felt in Ember. With no time to spare, Peace made a guess and pushed his fullest impression of love deep into the vortex of emotions.

It worked! Love was exactly the thing that the poor, tortured creature desired and needed. As Peace worked the concept deeper into its mind, the dragon slowly began to calm, its emotions becoming less troubled, its thoughts becoming clearer. Peace became vaguely aware that the creature, which had been roaring and pulling as though against invisible chains, was no longer struggling. Instead its eyes stared up into his, wide with surprise, pleading yet strangely trusting, as though experiencing the feeling of protection and belonging for the first time.

"Get off him!" someone yelled, and Peace was knocked back by a burly arm, losing his touch on the dragon's scales. The creature roared with surprise and tried to rush toward him, but suddenly men were all over it, grabbing hold of its horns and pulling it back. Peace picked himself up and managed to grab his sword off the ground.

"Stop!" he yelled in horror. "Stop it!"

But the men had already overpowered the dragon, wrestling its head to the ground; one of them was holding his hand upon its scales, speaking roughly to it. Peace rushed forward and fought the two men who tried to block his way. As he pushed past them however, he saw the dragon's eyes go from frightened, to passive, and then to wild and cruel. Peace desperately broke through and rushed toward the dragon, but already it was snarling like before and rising up into the air on its giant wings. Behind where it once stood, the gate was now open, and men were pouring through.

With no other choice, Peace turned and ran. All around him skirmishes broke out and the fighting became wild. Peace fought for all he was worth, not even knowing who it was that he was fighting. All was disorder and chaos, lit by the flaming walls and buildings. Peace had never been a great swordsman, but he fared slightly better as he fought left-handed, which caught most of his opponents off guard. It was impossible to tell which side was winning, and Peace did not have time to contemplate it; he was fighting for his life and knew little else.

Then suddenly, from behind, there came a great blast of fire and the man sparring him at that moment turned and fled. Peace spun around and saw against flickering flames the dark outline of a dragon hovering just above the ground on beating wings. As he watched, the beast landed hard and shot fire all around itself as though staking its ground. Peace's eyes widened, recognizing the maneuver.

"Ember," he whispered.

The great dragon was indeed his old companion. The flames between them cleared and Peace saw the firelight reflect dully against his green scales; the dancing shadows all around seemed to make the beast look bigger and darker than he had ever seemed before. Peace looked up and Ember stared into his eyes without recognition or mercy, growling through his large teeth.

At that moment a dark figure leapt from the dragon's back landing between them, crouched, with sword extended. Peace groaned and held his own sword at the ready.

"Deception."

"Aye," said the man, standing up.

The flames had died down a little, but Peace was able to make out the features of his face and the grin that he wore. Around them, the fighting became distant and indistinct. Peace eyed the situation carefully, looking briefly between man and dragon. Here was Ember; this was his chance! If only he could get around Deception.

Peace slowly began to circle to the right, careful to keep his sword extended. To his relief, Deception circled with him.

"You have a lot of guts coming here," Deception said, grinning wickedly. He eyed Peace's sword. "Ahh, I see that you have learned to fight with your left hand. How clever of you. What do you think, Ember? Shall we make his left the same as his right?"

The dragon grunted.

Peace kept his eyes on Deception. They had circled almost a quarter of the way.

Suddenly, Deception leapt forth and attacked wildly with his saber. Peace defended himself viciously, but then leapt back to buy more time. Deception stayed where he was and smiled.

"I'm surprised with you, Peace," he said as they started to circle again. "You fight hard, but what do you hope to achieve?"

He laughed wildly, extending his arms to gesture at the scene around them. "Is this what I get? I capture the very dragon of the Dragon Rider, and this is all the better you can do? I'm disappointed; I didn't expect to take your title so easily."

"You are no Rider," seethed Peace. "As long as I live, you can never be one."

Deception laughed. "Ahh, but I think that in order to be the Dragon Rider, one must actually possess a dragon to ride, no? And oh—you don't qualify anymore, do you?"

Peace bit his lip to hold back his rising temper. They had circled halfway; now he was the one between Ember and Deception. Feeling the presence of a hostile dragon behind him made Peace nervous, but he kept his eyes forward.

Now was his chance. Should he turn and quickly try to reclaim Ember? Would there be enough time?

But he never got to choose because suddenly Deception leapt for him, and Peace found himself fighting harder than he ever had in his life. They battled wildly and fiercely, spinning and ducking and blocking and thrusting. Deception laughed maniacally the whole time, always leaping clear of every sword swipe. Peace began to wonder how he had defeated him at all on the shore of World's End. He wondered if Deception had purposely allowed himself to be knocked aside, if the full skill of his enemy was far greater than he had known.

Then suddenly, in a movement too quick to fathom, Deception leapt backward into the air and as Peace lunged forward at him, a great tail swung under Deception's feet and knocked Peace flat on his back. His Link barely warned him in time to roll right as fire blasted to his left. Peace stopped his roll and tried to gather his bearings, wondering where he had dropped his sword.

A claw fell upon him from the darkness and pinned him to the ground! Peace struggled vainly under the pressure but stopped when he saw the eyes of a snarling dragon high above. From somewhere, Deception laughed wildly. "Very good, Ember! Very good indeed!"

Peace heard footsteps approaching him and felt desperately for his sword.

Deception's form came into view, dark and upside-down against the night sky. He smiled. "Really Peace, I expected more. I *wanted* more. Why can't I get a good opponent? All my planning and preparation, and I never even needed half of it."

"Be careful what you wish for," Peace grunted from under Ember's claw.

"Was this your plan? To come in with this pitiful crew and just *take* my dragon? I'm curious to know what you were expecting to do next. After you defeated me, destroyed my empire, and laid waste to my armies, were you just going to ask Ember to leave? Do you still think he wants you?"

Peace groaned under the weight. "He will never forget me. I know it."

"Ahh," said Deception. "So it's your faith that makes you so stupid. You still think that you can pull him away." He scratched his chin with his hand and appeared to think for a moment.

Finally, he looked down and smiled. "Ok, former Rider, I offer you a challenge." He looked up at the dragon. "Let him up, Ember."

The dragon reluctantly obeyed and stepped back. Peace got up, choking and trying to regain his breath. He spied his sword, but it was several feet away. He looked back toward Deception.

"All right," the man said, swinging his saber around carelessly, "my challenge is this. I will allow you one minute with Ember. There will be no interruptions, no distractions, no tricks; it will be just the two of you. If you can succeed in bringing him back, then I give my word that I will leave with my forces, and you will be free to head home with him. I'll let you both go without a fight, no questions asked."

Peace eyed him warily. "And if I cannot?"

Deception's smile faded. "Then I only ask you to consider what you are up against. I ask that you reconsider your futile mission, and that you consider packing up and going home while you still have your life."

Peace looked back and forth between the man and the dragon.

"Do we have a deal?" Deception asked.

Peace thought hard about it, knowing there had to be a trick somewhere, but he was unable to find it. "I agree."

"Good!" said Deception, grinning and taking a step back.

Peace turned to face Ember who look down upon him warily and growled.

"Now, now Ember," came Deception's voice. "Don't bite."

The dragon looked down for a few more seconds, and then slowly lowered his head to where Peace could reach, eyeing him distastefully. Peace swallowed hard and stepped forward; he closed his eyes, attempted to calm himself, and placed his hand on the dragon's snout.

Peace knew from the beginning that his mission was nearly hopeless. Though he probed, all that Ember's mind revealed to him was anger and loathing. He tried to search for that part he had felt before, the edge of Ember's memory that still trusted him, but he could not find it. No matter where he looked, all he felt was more anger, more hunger, and more desire. It was the same ravenous wanting he had sensed in him before—a desire for something that could not be identified, something that seemed to sparkle and dance around the edges of his consciousness while eluding its own name.

The more Peace searched, the more saddened he became; Ember's mind had changed. Where there was once joy there was now ambition. Where there was once peace, there was hunger. Where there was once nobility and love, there was pride and greed. Everything about him seemed devoid of care and compassion, and Peace wondered how Deception could have starved him of it in so little time. Peace tried desperately to reach out with love, like he had for the dragon at the gatehouse, but Ember's consciousness loathed it. He cared nothing for love now, preferring a strange hunger that wreaked a ravenous destruction throughout his mind.

"Ember, please," whispered Peace. "Come back. I forgive you for everything, just come back home; leave this man and let us ride together again, free and unburdened as before. Let me love you like I once did."

So Peace called, but Ember resisted completely. It was almost as though a strange force was blocking everything he did, shielding Ember's mind from him.

Peace withdrew his hand and backed away. The countenance before him was entirely unchanged; the dragon still growled, his eyes still piercing through Peace.

"Don't you see?" came Deception's voice. "This is hopeless! The beast you once knew is dead, my Curse killed him. You cannot reclaim him because there is nothing left to reclaim. He is mine now—you have been entirely forgotten!"

Peace stared dumbly ahead at the dragon; his fists clenched.

"You lie."

Deception laughed once again. "I only lie when it's my advantage to do so. If the truth will serve me just as well, I have no problem speaking it. It is you who lie—you lie to yourself! You keep fighting a battle that cannot be won. You lost! You've lost ever since you rejected your dragon at Watergate."

Deception walked from behind him and mounted Ember, sheathing his saber. "You have three days to leave," he said. "I'll admit that it's been fun watching you fail, and fail yet again, but now I grow tired of the game. Next time we meet, I will kill you—I'll kill you right in front of your precious dragon as he looks on." He smiled and turned Ember away.

Around him, Peace was vaguely aware that the fighting had stopped and that the invading soldiers were heading back out of the gate.

Deception paused momentarily. "I hope for your sake that we do not meet again on this shore. I hope that for once you will listen to some sound advice."

Then with a blast of wind Ember was airborne, flapping his wings and flying out into the night. All around, stillness settled in. Deception had left, his army had left, his dragons had left; all that remained was a troop of injured, despairing soldiers, and the ruins of a town called Hope.

Peace turned sorrowfully away from it all and wandered toward the central tower. He heard stumbling footsteps and turned to see his captain from the voyage limping toward him.

"My prince," he said. "I've received word from the soldiers; Defiance was killed in the attack."

Peace turned away as grief overwhelmed him. Tears formed in his eyes.

"What are we going to do?" he heard the captain say. "Should we ready the ship to depart?"

Peace stopped. He was looking at the ground, but now his fists were clenched and his face was hard. His head snapped back up, anger in his eyes. "Yes," he said. "Prepare the ship to sail immediately. But I will not be on it."

"But my prince," protested the captain. "What can you possibly hope to do?"

"I will follow the only course of action left open to me."

"And what is that?" the captain asked.

Peace looked hard out at the sea. "I must call for Justice."

The captain's eyes widened. "Justice? But my prince, he'll kill Ember. You know that he will."

"I know," said Peace, his eyes softening, "and I'll try to reason with him if I can. But if that's the price to save Ember from that...that monster, then I must accept it. Justice is the only one who can help us now."

# 3

## And Judgment Rains Down from the Skies

Night found Ember in his prison cell, dreaming once again. Around him the darkness was damp and quiet, only the occasional drip of water from a distant corridor broke the silence. But still the dragon was uneasy. He tossed and shifted in his sleep as he found himself reliving an event of his past—one so distant that it took him back to the days before the Sending Out, when he was still being trained as the Rider's dragon...

*Ember leapt nimbly through the grass as he attempted to keep up with Glory. She was many years older than he, and each of her steps required nearly four of his own to stay at her side. They soon came to an open field near the top of a hill where they could see for miles and look down at the forest at the edge of Highland's immediate territory. Above them the sky was blue and clear.*

*"Will we be flying today?" Ember asked excitedly. He bounded out and around the great dragon until he was in front of her. He looked like a young kitten in her presence.*

"Yes, we will," said Glory calmly with a hint of playfulness in her eyes. "But there is something I want to talk to you about first."

"What is it?" asked Ember eagerly.

"There is a common mistake that young dragons make early in their service to their Rider. I was prone to it myself, and I want you to be better prepared. The fact of the matter is, most young dragons see themselves as their Rider's protector, as if they were a giant bodyguard."

"But isn't that what I am?" asked Ember cocking his head. He turned to look down the hillside. "I think he needs one."

Glory looked down the hill as well and saw Peace sparing with Justice out in the open field.

"Keep your sword up!" he was shouting as Peace ducked and clumsily blocked his brother's controlled swings. "Yes, you are quick and agile, but that is not enough to save you in battle. Your sword must be quick too! Use your blade, not your feet. Try to block me!"

The two dragons watched in amusement as Justice continued to best his brother despite his attempts to hold himself back.

"I do love him," said Ember as he watched, "but he is not the best swordsman. Shouldn't I be his protector?"

"Yes, you certainly should," said Glory. "The problem however comes when a young dragon takes too much pride in that responsibility. Yes, you should protect him from harm; but remember that most of the conflicts you encounter will not require aggression to solve. The two of you are to try and resolve all problems in a peaceful manner, if possible. Don't be too quick to 'protect' your Rider; do so only as far as it aids him in his job."

"Of course," said Ember, bowing his head. "But there are times where we will have to fight, are there not? How should I know the difference?"

"Follow your Rider. Let him decide when you should attack and when you should not. Follow his command, and all will be right."

"But what if we are attacked?" said Ember, excitement rising in his eyes. "If we are attacked by a score of men, what should I do? Should I use fire?"

Glory laughed quietly. "Young ones always wish to use their fire; it seems to be their weapon of choice. But I would recommend you avoid it for two reasons. First of all, most often it will not be your goal to kill the people attacking you, but only to fight them off. Use fire only when you are sure that Peace wishes them to be destroyed.

"The second reason, however, is one of tactics. All dragons have a limited amount of fire within them. It increases over the years and can be replenished through eating, but in the heat of battle you must be careful never to run out. Many people will fear your fire more than anything else. It is better to not use it and keep them in fear, then to use it all and run out, allowing enemies to attack more boldly."

Ember looked at his mentor a little disappointed. "Then what should I do if we are attacked?"

"First, try to frighten them. In most places, the very presence of the Dragon Rider has earned enough respect to suppress whole armies. If you cannot frighten them with your presence, however, focus on the other weapons at your disposal. Teeth, claws, and tail when used properly can deal far more damage than fire. Of course, you can still blast your assailants with flame if you need to but use it as a last resort, and as a means of creating fear and disorder. Your tail can be especially useful when facing a large number of people—you'd be surprised how many you can knock over at once. Avoid snapping and biting, however, unless you face a single assailant, and one as big as you. And above all, you must never forget your greatest asset."

"And what is that?" asked Ember eagerly.

"Your wings," said Glory, and with a leap that shook the ground she launched herself into the air, her wings beating slowly and powerfully as she rose. Ember quickly leapt up to follow her, his wings beating much faster on account of their smaller size. The big, midnight-black dragon rose several hundred feet above ground and then hovered. Ember quickly rose and tried to stay level with her.

"Flight is your greatest ally," she said. "It gives you a tactical advantage and can allow you to escape from nearly any conflict. No other animal aside from a griffin has the ability to both fly and fight on the ground as we do. Use these gifts wisely."

"Do you think I will ever need to fight while in the air?"

"There are very few dangers that can reach you when you are up here. I suppose there is a chance you may encounter a wild griffin in your travels, but it is rare that they will directly attack a dragon unless they have lost their minds. There are also wild dragons up north, but I see no reason why you should ever be there. I advise you against fighting with your own kind—it can be dangerous and will likely have no bearing on your mission."

"Have you ever fought another dragon?" asked Ember.

Glory smiled. "Yes. Back when I was much younger I fought two at the same time during our mission to the Shadowlands." The younger dragon stared up at her in awe and she chuckled. "I beat them; they were both bigger than me, but I beat them still. Being a Rider's dragon, I was calmer and more focused of mind than our wilder and more savage kin. The King also helped, and it is thanks to him that I survived."

"What should I do if I encounter an aggressive dragon?"

"I should hope you never do, but over all you must be careful to protect your wings. Shield them from fire, because if they are harmed, you will fall from the sky. Fold them against your sides if necessary—even if it means dropping suddenly—and go for your opponent's wings."

"Can I try that now?" asked Ember eagerly.

Glory chuckled. "You are very daring, my young one. Be careful that you do not allow your dreams and fantasies to carry you away. Yes, we can practice. Try and reach one of my wings if you can."

Ember immediately dove at the command, spinning and diving down through the air before shooting up for the great dragon's left wing. He quickly had to dodge her left claw and was forced to bank away before turning and striking again. Twice he tried and twice Glory fended him off, always orienting herself in midair to face him without changing her position greatly. Ember soon grew tired and broke off his attack, flying out in front and looking at her scornfully. Glory laughed.

"Very good!" she said. "You have speed, as I once did. Use that to your advantage."

"Are you not as fast as you once were?" asked Ember.

"No, but I do not need to be. With time we become slower, but our strength and stamina increase. I could outlast several dragons your size in battle. And every year I grow stronger, as you will too."

"Do we always grow stronger?" asked Ember. "Is there ever a time when we stop growing?"

Glory's eyes sparkled as she smiled. "Yes, but you do not need to fear that day. Because we are bonded to Riders, we will die shortly after they do. Humans live much shorter lives than dragons, so dying with them allows us to escape the effects of old age."

"So, our Riders shorten our lifespan?" asked Ember with concern. "Will I not live out my full life because of Peace?"

"It depends on what you call life. Yes, you will not live as long, but I personally count it no loss to sacrifice my weaker years to live my best in service to my Rider. You will quickly learn, my dear Ember, that life, no matter how long, is not worth living without a master, without someone to devote yourself to. Protect Peace with your life. It is better for you to die at his side, than to live on after his death. Remember that my young Ember...."

In his cell, Ember came suddenly awake with a growl in his throat and a snarl on his face.

* * *

The sun was rising in the east as Justice watched the King fasten his battle armor. He stood in the castle courtyard with his subjects and the remainder of his armies behind him. To his left stood Glory, black as midnight and as large and magnificent as ever; her glossy scales shimmered in the morning light as she sniffed the air patiently, waiting for her Rider.

In front of them stood the enormous gate of the outer wall which encircled the castle; beyond that gate lay only the endless expanse of the invading army. In the sky above, nine dragons with their riders hovered in attack formation, waiting for the King to take to the skies. They could have struck long before but there was an eerie calmness and reverence that accompanied the King's presence, and neither side seemed willing to break it.

Justice watched sadly as his father strapped the Sword of the Kings to his side and mounted his dragon. He approached his father slowly, and the stillness of the air made his voice nearly a whisper.

"You don't have to do this."

The King turned to him.

"I know," he said, and then smiled. "You have done marvelously, my son. You fought hard and gave all you had for this kingdom. Now it is time for me to fight for my subjects."

Justice shook his head sadly. "But I have failed you. I tried to defend the people and could not. It should never have come to this."

The King reached down and placed his hand on Justice's head. "You did not fail, my son. You fought a battle that was impossible to win, and yet you did not give up. The courage you showed was the courage of kings." He sat back up and drew his great sword, sending the ringing sound of steel through the air. "Besides," he said, "it was always my design to ride out into battle myself. Even if you had succeeded in driving them away, I still would have done so."

Justice took a step back, shaking his head. "But why?" he asked. "If it was always your intention to fight, then why did you wait so long? There were other, more fortified defenses and positions we could've fought for. Why did you let these invaders take nearly your entire kingdom?"

"The kingdom matters not to me if my subjects are safe," the King said, taking a quick glance behind at his people watching them. Then he looked forward toward the great army and its dragons. His face saddened. "I held back for the sake of the six nations that attack us. I wanted to give them a chance before I rode out against them."

"A chance?" said Justice with surprise. "A chance for what?"

The King raised his sword high.

"For repentance," he said. And then the ground shook with a mighty rumble as Glory leapt into the air, unfolding massive wings that blocked out the rising sun as she rose toward the waiting dragons above.

It was only then that Justice understood. He watched with amazement as the King flew higher, Glory dwarfing the nine smaller dragons. The three in front attacked first, shooting toward the King with great speed, but Glory bathed the middle one in a river of fire and then banked sharply to left, striking another of the dragons with her great tail and breaking its neck.

The third dragon eluded Glory's range of vision and dove for her wing, but just then the King leapt from his mount and landed atop the smaller dragon, killing its rider and hacking the neck with his great sword. His weapon could not pierce the scales, but its very weight was enough to crush the bone beneath, and in a moment that dragon too was spinning toward the ground. The King leapt from it and Glory caught him easily upon her back, his intention having been relayed through the Link.

Then the other six dragons attacked at once, diving and striking at every angle. They seemed unable, however, to overpower the King's mount. Glory fought back forcefully; she was not as fast as the smaller dragons, but each successful blow meant death. They tried to outflank her, but the King seemed to always be there, leaping from one dragon to another with the ease of a dancer and relaying everything he saw back to Glory, so that she knew the positions of even the dragons she could not see.

Tooth, tail, and claw clashed against scales; fire blazed in the sky; the roars and screeches of angry dragons echoed all around. But eventually the attack began to fall into disorder. Two more of the dragons had been killed and the others, to avoid serious injury, had employed such a dizzying display of aerobatic twists and dives in order to do so, that their riders had all either fallen or been thrown off.

Without humans to guide them, the dragons began to strike more wildly and recklessly, their actions being fueled by fear rather than any actual desire to kill. The King saw this, and made a leap back onto Glory, who hovered in place and began to beat the air forcefully with her giant wings. The blasts of air were more than enough to push back and scatter the four smaller dragons; they were hurled through the air, flapping desperately to regain control before panicking and fleeing in different directions.

With his airborne assailants thwarted, the King pointed his sword at the ground and Glory swooped downward toward the enemy soldiers outside the gate. Upon seeing this, Justice grinned. He drew his katana and called out, "To me, men of Highland! Open the gate! Charge!"

Immediately, the war-beaten army of Highland cheered, drew their weapons, and charged after him shouting and hollering. The gate was opened, and through it Justice looked just in time to see Glory land powerfully on the other side with the force of an earthquake. The great dragon roared at the shaken ranks of the invading army and blasted fire around in a half circle, forcing them to back up. The King leapt down from her side and brandished the Sword of the Kings.

Justice rushed through the gate and with both of his weapons drawn he plunged into the enemy ranks alongside his father, the soldiers of Highland just behind him. Their enemies, though they numbered far greater, panicked. They had expected to watch the King die in the battle in the sky. The sudden turn of events had not given them enough time to prepare; many of their men were killed before they could form ranks again to hold their ground.

Justice battled fiercely, but his heart sank when he saw the four dragons regroup in the skies and prepare to dive toward them. With no visible prompting, Glory took off, shaking the ground, to engage the dragons above.

The fighting became hard and fierce, but the soldiers of Highland were now alongside their King while the invaders were still trying to overcome panic and disorder. The combined skills of the King and Justice were more than any of them could overcome, and their growing fear was heightened when Glory hurled a dead dragon from the sky into the middle of their forces, crushing many men.

Soon their nerve broke completely, and the enemy troops began to run back toward a gate they had already conquered in the outer wall. But only half of them had made it through before Glory landed hard in the gateway, roaring and blasting fire in the faces of the retreating force.

With the King's dragon before them and the King himself behind, most of the invaders cried out and dropped to their knees, their hands in the air. Those who did not surrender were quickly killed off, and the remainder of the men who had made it through the gate decided to abandon their comrades rather than face the wrath of the King's great mount. In the skies above, the three remaining dragons also fled, two very injured.

The King gave orders to his men regarding the prisoners and then made his way toward his dragon, breathing heavily. Glory was also breathing hard and bleeding in several places along her unprotected neck and belly. The King gently stroked her scales, speaking softly to her.

Justice approached. "That was unbelievable! I'm sorry that I ever doubted you."

The King smiled. "Now you know why Highland has never been taken. I learned much while being the Dragon Rider, but I learned still more afterward."

"Shall we pursue the rest of them?" Justice asked, his katana still drawn. The King shook his head but did not turn away from Glory.

"No," he said, "I want to give the rest of them a chance to surrender before we attack."

"Do we plan on keeping even more of them alive; the very people who have dared to attack our nation?"

"Yes," said the King. "Of course, they will not receive as good a treatment as those who surrendered here, just as those who surrendered here will not be treated as well as those who surrendered before. But all will keep their lives."

"Why?" asked Justice angrily. "They don't deserve a second chance!"

"I know," the King said softly, almost more to Glory than to Justice. "But I want to give them one."

Justice stabbed his sword into the ground. "But they will attack again, you know that."

"Yes, they will. They have seen that they are outmatched, but they will still try again. No doubt next time they will try to use some trick or other scheme, but it will fail. Many of them will still refuse to surrender, their pride and fear forcing them on against impossible odds, but still, I will wait." He turned to face Justice.

"My son, you have now seen my power. Highland is safe, and soon the remains of this invasion will be eliminated. I will take care of what is still left to be done here; you, however, have a much harder mission."

"Mission? What mission do I have?" asked Justice.

The King turned toward the Western Sea. "At this very moment, the ship Peace took to the Shadowlands is approaching at full speed with a minimal crew. It bears one message: Bring Justice."

Justice looked at his father with confusion. "If the ship is still out at sea, how can you know?"

"I expect it," said the King. "I knew that once Peace landed, he would likely be attacked by Deception. After his inevitable defeat, he would find himself forced to call for help. I would be unable to leave my kingdom, especially with it under attack, and so you would be the only one he could think to summon."

"But how can he...what does he expect me to do? Only a fool would challenge Deception in his own country."

"And yet your brother does so. You fought the impossible here, and now Peace is doing it there. He needs you."

"To do what? Rescue that condemned dragon of his? Even if we did reclaim it, the penalty for its treason is death. You know that don't you?"

The King bowed his head sadly. "Yes, I do...but only if Ember has committed treason willingly. There may be more to this than you realize."

"But the dragon fights alongside Deception, whether it does so willingly or not. It may be impossible to kill one without destroying the other."

"I know," said the King. "But perhaps the very fact that Peace has called for you means that he is starting to accept it. He will still want to rescue his companion, but perhaps his sees death as a better fate than affliction."

"But he still won't listen to me," said Justice. "How can we possibly work together?"

The King put his hand on his shoulder. "Justice, you need to learn from your brother just as he must learn from you. Go, and do what you can; I place you in charge of the mission. You may kill or redeem Ember at your discretion—I only ask that you listen to Peace and try to understand him. I know that you will do what is right."

The King stood up and accepted a saddlebag handed to him by a messenger. "You must go swiftly," he said. "Take the fastest ship you can and do not overburden it with soldiers. You must reach Peace as soon as possible."

Justice stepped back. "I am not ready for this mission," he said.

The King nodded, "I know, but I will not send you unprepared. I have three things for you before you leave."

Justice looked up, and the King's face was stern.

"The first is a warning. Last night was the new moon. By the time of the full moon, I will have gathered my forces and brought them to the Shadowlands."

"Then you will fight with us?" asked Justice.

"Yes, but you must go before me. I will land in the north near a great battlefield; you have until the night of the full moon to meet me there. While the moon is not yet full, I will show mercy to all who come. Afterward however, I will attack and destroy all that I encounter. Ensure that you and your party are with me before that night."

Justice nodded.

"The second thing I must give you is this." The King pulled a letter from the saddlebag he had been given. It was sealed with his own seal. "While I hope you will never need to use it, I give this to you for the hour of greatest need. When you are at your wit's end, and when you cannot see how to go on, read this—I believe it will provide help."

Justice accepted it but looked at the letter curiously. "How can you know the nature of the situation that will cause me to open it?" he asked.

The King smiled. "There are very few to choose from; do not worry."

Then removing his own Link, the King looked up at Glory.

"The last thing I have for you is this," he held out the Link to Justice. "I want you to put this on for a moment."

Justice backed away, "I am forbidden to—"

"I give you my permission. Do not fear."

Carefully, Justice took the treasure and placed it around his neck.

Justice had never worn a Link before, and so the sensation of perceiving another's thoughts and feelings was an unexpected shock. He spun around and faced Glory, the great and powerful dragon whose mind was now completely open to him. He could sense everything about her: what she loved, what she feared; her vulnerabilities and longings; her nightmares and desires. Yet Glory did not hold anything back. She poured forth herself willingly and contentedly.

The King held out his hand and Justice returned the Link. The mental connection vanished.

"Do you see how Glory gives herself to you?" he asked, looking up at the dragon.

Justice nodded.

"You know everything about her," said the King. "You could destroy her if you wanted, and still, she gives you herself. That is the deepest extent of love between a dragon and its Rider. That is the way it should've been with Peace and Ember."

The King turned to face Justice. "I needed you to understand what he lost; he gave himself to that dragon and it betrayed him. But even still, Peace has retained enough love to continue searching, hoping that there exists out there the Ember he once knew. That is what makes him so persistent. That is also why he appears so foolish. As you go about your mission, remember that—remember how it was supposed to be."

Justice nodded and the King smiled. "Good; now quickly organize your ship. Whether it be that Peace must kill or save Ember, I believe he will need your help to do it."

# 4

Thunder Rumbles

Ruthless was surprised to see Ember in the throne room when he stepped in. Deception was kneeling beside the dragon, stroking the scales of its neck, and whispering softly to it. Ruthless moved forward quietly and was able to catch some of his words.

"...that is why so few people think your kind exists, why you have no natural habitats. All other animals belong to this earth—they have purposes that fit together, that combine to form the interworking of the great and complex machine. But your only purpose, my dear Ember, is to destroy; that is what you were created for, what all dragons are created for. Like humans you are an alien to this world. You see, my Ember, neither of us have any place in nature; we do not contribute to it, we only harm it. It's funny, isn't it, that we were ever created at all."

Ruthless cleared his throat. Deception ceased talking but did not look up.

"Are you all right, sire?"

Deception continued to stroke the dragon's scales. Ember stared straight ahead, his eyes looked content but somehow still fiery and hungry.

"Ember is dying," said Deception quietly.

Ruthless was struck. There was no pain or regret in his master's voice; it was as if he was only stating a fact. The dragon did not react at all; it appeared hypnotized.

"I'm sorry, what did you say?"

Deception slowly got up and turned to face him. "I said he is dying. The Curse is ravaging his mind. He has only about a week to live, perhaps two."

"And this does not bother you?" asked Ruthless tentatively.

Deception smiled and shook his head.

"Of course not. I knew this would happen; it's the price of using an enchantment so powerful. I knew that the hunger that burns inside Ember would eventually destroy him. I wanted to have the Dragon Rider Pact tear itself apart—to use it as a weapon against Highland. And then after all that, to have the very dragon I used, the last remnant of the old age, destroy itself with its own savagery. It is all part of my plan."

He turned back to Ember and looked at him longingly. "Besides," he added, "the star that burns half as long burns twice as bright."

He stared at the dragon for a few more moments and then turned to look up at Ruthless. "I believe that you bring me news regarding its former Rider?"

"Yes," said Ruthless. "Peace has not left. In fact, another ship lies docked next to his own. I believe that he called for reinforcements."

Deception shook his head sadly and turned to Ember. "It's a pity, really. He was supposed to die like a common soldier among his people when I came back. I didn't count on him being stubborn and blind." He sighed. "I guess however, that he has chosen his fate. We don't have time to play around anymore."

He looked back toward Ruthless. "Prepare your men, we will attack Hope tomorrow at noon; this time, we kill everyone."

Ruthless smiled and bowed slightly. "Yes, my lord. It will be done immediately."

He turned and left. Deception smiled to himself, and then resumed stroking Ember.

"Don't worry my dear Ember; your old Rider will soon plague you no more. Tomorrow, you will at last be made completely free." He smiled again and rested his head against the dragon's neck.

"My Ember, my dear, dying Ember."

* * *

Peace walked through the city of Hope, Justice his brother at his side. "I am so glad you came," Peace said with relief in his voice. "I didn't think you would have enough time after receiving the message."

"Yes, well, I had a head start. The King was able to anticipate your request."

"Is he all right?" asked Peace. "How did Highland fare against the attack?"

"Highland was never in any danger. The King could have taken their army singlehandedly. He has little to fear from Deception."

"Good. Then perhaps we can relax a little. Deception cannot hope to overcome him."

"Perhaps not, but it will not matter if he kills you here. You are the heir; that is why I came to protect you."

"I thought you came because you wanted to see Deception killed by your own blade."

Justice smiled wryly. "I do admit that was also a part of it. It is my goal, while I am here, to ensure that Deception pays for his crimes."

Peace smiled too, but falteringly. He was hesitant to bring up a subject that he knew the two of them would disagree on.

"What of Ember?" he asked. "It was my mission to bring him back."

Justice's face turned hard, and he looked ahead. "I am here to deal with Deception; Ember matters little to me except for how he may hinder me in that goal."

Peace tried to draw hope from his brother's resolve. It didn't seem like he was set on killing Ember, at least not for now. "Ember will cause you no problems if we can reclaim him," he said cautiously.

"Neither will he if he is dead."

Peace's hopes immediately fell.

After a few moments however, he said, "But if we have the chance, would you let me reclaim him?"

Justice sighed. "As long as it does not hinder my pursuit of Deception, I care not what you do with your dragon. He is none of my concern."

"But he should be; he is part of the Dragon Rider Pact, and so his Rider is heir to the throne. If I die, then his new master will become the next king."

"You will not die," said Justice firmly. "Not as long as I am here."

"Even so," said Peace tentatively, "I want you to have this." He held out a sealed letter to his brother. Justice looked at it suspiciously. "Please take it," Peace continued. "I want you to open it in the event of my death or capture."

Justice shook his head. "No, you will not die here on my watch; keep it."

"Please, I need you to—"

"No!" said Justice sharply. "Keep it, as a promise. Nothing will happen to you; I will not allow it."

Peace nodded, but there seemed to be tears in his eyes. "Very well, my brother; see to the defenses." Then he turned and headed off toward his tent. Justice stopped to watch him go, but then grunted and moved on.

He walked for several minutes before his two most trusted generals, Courage and Determination, approached. They both saluted him; Justice nodded in return.

"How is the city?" he asked.

Determination answered. "Many of the buildings have been burned, but the walls are still solid. Deception managed to open the gates from the inside, so none were broken down."

"Very good," said Justice, quite satisfied. "When do we expect the attack?"

"Deception told Peace that he had three days to leave," said Courage. "Tonight will end the third day, and so Deception will likely gather his forces and attack under the cover of night tomorrow."

"Very good," said Justice nodding. "We will have until then to prepare."

"Exactly how will we prepare?" asked Courage. "How can we defend against Deception's forces?"

Justice looked up toward the central tower for a moment, but then bowed his head.

"I'm afraid I don't know. As of yet, I don't have a plan."

* * *

That night, Peace got little sleep. He stayed awake long into the night, sitting on his bed and wondering what was to become of them all. What would become of him? What would become of Ember? A tear rolled down from his eye.

From the darkness came a quiet sound and Peace looked up to see a small cat approaching him. It must have once belonged to someone because it allowed itself to be picked up without complaint.

"Was your owner killed in the attack?" Peace asked quietly. He hugged the cat close, and it purred, rubbing its head against his chest. Peace smiled sadly and stroked it with a gentle hand. "We've both lost someone we loved, haven't we?" The cat continued to purr, and he sighed. There was once a time when he had held Ember like this.

Peace leaned back against the bed and continued to draw his hand through the soft fur. It felt nice, comforting, almost as if it could smooth away all his troubles. Almost.

Peace looked up and stared blankly through the opening in his tent at a flickering campfire outside. In the dancing colors of red and orange he imagined he saw shapes, which took the form of memories. He saw a little dragon, terrified by the thunder of an oncoming storm, rushing through a palace to find its master. He watched as it found the form of a boy and leapt into his arms, burying its head against his chest. The boy stroked the trembling creature and took it to a sheltered corner, whispering soothing words to it until it calmed in his arms.

Peace blinked and the fire seemed to change. He saw the boy in bed, sick with flaming fever, shivering against the cold. He watched as the little dragon leapt up upon the blankets, nosed its way under them, and snuggled close the boy's heart. The boy slowly wrapped his arms around it and the dragon purred, rubbing against its master's burning skin.

The image flickered and was replaced by another. This time the dragon was outside at night. It had grown quite a bit larger but suffered from a virus that drained its strength. Beside its head sat the boy, his arms wrapped around its neck and his cheek pressed against its scales.

Again it flickered, and he saw the boy and the dragon flying together over the streets and houses of their home city. It changed again, and then again, bringing with it waves of memories. He saw the boy and the dragon riding out for the first night with their Links, exploring forests, flying over rivers, standing at the top of great mountains. He saw the dragon challenging a lion bigger than itself to protect its master; he saw the two of them playing with Glory, the King's dragon; he saw them in the throne room; he saw them the night after the Sending Out; he saw them in the wilderness, in towns, in kingdoms. Always they protected each other, always they helped each other, always wherever they went they were at each other's side.

Peace sighed deeply and a tear rolled down his cheek.

"I loved you," he whispered. "I loved you with all my heart and I had thought...I had thought that you loved me the same."

The cat stirred slightly in his arms, then got up, jumped to his bed, and curled up at its foot. Peace looked at his empty hands and then buried his face in them.

"My Eldar; my poor, deceived Eldar. Why do you resist me? You're lost in a dangerous land; why do you not allow yourself to be saved?"

* * *

Peace was unable to fall asleep until very late that night, but when at last he did so, his dreams tortured him.

*He saw himself standing on a wide plateau, and he saw Ember and Justice fighting before him. His dragon's eyes were as wild and merciless as ever, but his brother seemed even more so. He watched with horror as Ember tried to pounce again and again upon his smaller, nimbler opponent. He always just barely missed his target while Justice, spinning and ducking out of the way just in time, scored several minor hits upon the unprotected sides of Ember's legs. With each hit, the dragon roared and became even wilder. His brother was undaunted and fearless.*

*Peace, desperate, tried to step forward to quell the fight; but suddenly Deception was standing in his way.*

*"I can't allow you to do that," he said, smiling like he always did.*

*"Get out of my way you murderous, thieving dragon slayer!" Peace screamed.*

*Deception only laughed. "Dragon Slayer? I have outgrown that title."*

*He spread out his arms. "I am the Dragon Tamer! If you wish to see the true Dragon Slayer, then you need only to look before you." He gestured and Peace saw that his dragon was nearly frantic now. He was bleeding in several places and the charred rocks told of his many failed attempts to blast his assailant with fire.*

*Justice was untiring, and as the fight continued, he seemed to only get faster and more elusive. Then, suddenly, Ember scored a hit. It was a wild, blind swipe of his right foreclaw, but it was enough force to knock Justice several feet away to the ground, sending his dagger spinning into the darkness and his katana clattering across the rocks.*

*Justice picked himself up and spotted his sword. Ember stood before him, crouched and ready to spring. It would have been wise for the dragon to simply destroy him with flame from a distance, but it was clear from his eyes that Ember was too enraged to think of that.*

*Justice dove for his sword, rolling across the ground, and managed to get his fingers around the handle. Behind him, Ember pounced, leaping like a tiger, claws extended to crush his victim. Sensing the attack, Justice, in one smooth motion, spun around, rising up on one knee as he did so, and lifted his blade point to impale Ember's heart as he fell upon him.*

*Peace let out a scream that produced no sound. He watched as the dragon landed upon his brother and as the sword pierced its chest.*

With a gasp, Peace jerked awake, disturbing the cat sleeping at the foot of his bed. With a groan he allowed himself to fall back, wiping the sweat from his brow. Oh, what had he done? What was he thinking to have asked Justice here? Through the flaps of his tent, Peace saw that it was already day, perhaps already a good deal into the morning. Feverishly, he got up, dressed, and moved out into the open air. He had to find Justice before it was too late. He looked around and immediately set out in search of his brother.

Above him, the sun reached its peak in the sky, signaling the imminent noon.

* * *

Justice walked through camp with a gruff manner. It was nearly midday, and he still had no idea what he was going to do. Additionally, he had woken up that morning to find Peace's letter on his desk. He had finally taken it, deciding that if his brother was so persistent, it must mean a lot to him; but he felt a foreboding in the air, as if somehow it sealed Peace's doom by doing so.

He was walking among the tents, talking with Determination who had joined him, when he heard the alarm. Three blasts upon the horn. With near panic, Justice whirled around and saw his men jumping up and grabbing their weapons. From the direction of the wall, he saw Courage running to them.

"Sire!" he said, panting. "Attackers are coming! Dragons, and horsemen—they'll be here in only a few minutes."

"I thought you said that Deception wouldn't come until tonight!" gasped Justice with disbelief.

"A tactical misjudgment on my part. I thought he would wait for the cover of darkness, like before."

Justice fumed and paced the ground restlessly. So, Deception had chosen surprise and speed over a strategic advance—that meant he was probably confident of his forces and not expecting much resistance. *Think! How can I use this to my advantage?* Deception was probably expecting the battle to be quick and decisive. His army was no doubt great in strength and numbers. *Too many to overcome. Can I throw them into panic?* They had dragons too; they would be just as devastating here as in Highland. *That is where their bravery lies. How do I overcome dragons?* Nothing had succeeded before. *Think! What do we have to work with?* Justice shut his eyes tightly and pulled his hair, trying to concentrate.

Then his eyes snapped open. "Skylances!" he exclaimed.

He turned to Courage. "How many skylances are in this city?"

"There's one atop the tower, sire, and about six or seven more stored in its base."

"I need them now!" shouted Justice, grabbing the general by the shoulders. "Get them loaded and mobilized immediately; prepare a squad of the finest marksmen—ask those native to this city. Tell them, when I blow twice on the horn they should move those crossbows out into the open and shoot every one of those flying beasts out of the sky."

Courage nodded boldly and immediately turned to do as he was commanded. Justice turned to Determination.

"Determination, I need you to organize the troops. I want all archers up on the battlements, shooting every dragon they can. Tell them to aim for the wings. Send all the rest of the soldiers to guard the gatehouse. It *must not* be taken again."

Determination also nodded, his face hard and set, and began shouting orders to the troops. Justice turned to find his brother.

* * *

The attack had not yet begun when Justice located Peace and ushered him into the great stone tower along with two other soldiers. As soon as they began to climb however, screams, shouts, and exploding fire began to echo all around them. The walls of the tower protected them, at least momentarily, but even still Peace felt his stomach turning. On the stairs ahead of him marched Justice, and behind came the two soldiers.

As they climbed, Peace remained quiet. But as they neared the top, he tentatively broke the silence. "What makes you so determined to climb this tower? It is because of the view it affords of the city?"

"I seek it because it is relatively the safest place to be right now, and also because of its skylance."

Peace shivered. He understood that the danger of the situation forced his brother to desperate measures, but still he hated to see any of the magnificent flying beasts injured or killed.

"There's a better way than shooting the dragons," he said. "I reclaimed one before. During the last attack, I touched one and brought it out of the control of its rider. I think that I can do it again."

"You were unable to do that with Ember."

"Ember felt different; I believe Deception did something unusual to him. But the others can still be redeemed. Wouldn't it be better if we could get the dragons to join our side rather than having to kill them?"

"I cannot put you in that type of danger," said Justice firmly. "Besides, it would be near impossible to get one to land long enough for you to do anything."

They reached the top and Justice poked his head out of the trapdoor. Peace followed and soon found himself looking down upon the besieged flaming city. All around dragons swooped and roared and breathed fire down upon the fleeing people. Determination was barely managing to hold the gate, his resolve and firm mindset the only things keeping his men from falling into complete panic and disorder as flames exploded around them. Everywhere, the town was being ravaged and pillaged by the flying beasts.

"They're searching for you," said Justice grimly as he started to draw back the bowstring of the skylance with the help of the two soldiers. The giant crossbow was mounted on a tall platform that allowed it to spin around in a complete circle and tilt up and down so that it could be aimed at nearly any target. Peace swallowed hard when he saw the deadly device; he thought it looked sickening.

"Are you sure this will even be any good?" he asked. "You've ridden Ember before; you know that dragons can dodge the bolts."

Justice locked the string into place and lifted a giant arrow off a supply rack nearby. "Yes, but that is when they are expecting them. You didn't use this in the last attack, so it is likely they will not suspect it now. My first arrow should catch them completely unaware."

"But what then?" asked Peace desperately. "There are dozens of dragons out there. What can you hope to do with one arrow?" Justice set the bolt in its place and spun the crossbow around, taking aim.

"We take out their leader."

Peace spun to look at where the deadly arrow pointed and saw Ember, with Deception upon his back. They were a short way off, concentrating their attention on the progress of the battle. Ember was hovering vertically in the air on large, lazy beats of his wings, his unprotected chest turned toward them, giving Justice a clear shot.

"No! Stop!" cried Peace. "Don't do that!"

Justice eyed his target through the sights and placed his hand on the firing lever.

"I have to, it's the only way."

"No, please!" yelled Peace, flinging himself at his brother. Justice hollered to the soldiers, and they dragged Peace back to the wall.

"I dreamed this would happen," Peace continued to yell franticly. "You can't do it! I came all this way to save him! Why did even you bring me up here? Just to see him murdered before my eyes?"

Justice turned to look at him, his eyes blazed fierce and cold. "I am sorry, my brother. But that man Deception has killed our people, attacked Highland, and destroyed the peace of Tarenthia. Pain, lies, and destruction were his choice weapons and right now we have a chance to put an end to him, to stop this string of injustice! In one moment he could be killed, and everything could be put right!"

"Then kill the man, not my dragon!"

"The dragon protects our enemy!" shouted Justice, his eyes blazing. "Why should he be allowed to live?"

"I want to give him another chance!" begged Peace. "I have to see him sane again. Injure him if you must; bring him down so that I can talk to him, but please don't kill him!"

"We can't be sure of him landing inside the city walls; and even if he did, he would only cause widespread panic and disorder," said Justice, turning back to the aiming sights. "Killing a dragon is hard; capturing one is nearly impossible. There is no way that we could contain him safely enough for you to get near him." He put his hand on the lever again.

"I beg you," whispered Peace pleadingly. "Please..."

Justice gritted his teeth and aimed the point of his arrow at Ember's heart. But he couldn't get his brother's voice out of his mind. It did seem so wrong, so cruel, for Peace to watch the death of his own dragon.

Justice grumbled. But this was his chance! In one strike Deception could be killed and it would all be over! All it would take was one pull of a lever; he might never get a chance like this again. He turned briefly to look at his brother who stared at him beseechingly, and turned back. He rotated the crossbow slightly to the left so that it pointed at Ember's wing instead, and fired.

* * *

Deception had been leading Ember slowly across the city, scanning the ground for any sign of Peace, when they flew too close to the battlements. Several archers had shot at them from below, and Ember pulled to the side to avoid the arrows when it happened. A bolt, fired from a skylance, shot right past them directly where Ember's right wing had been only a second before. Deception spun his mount around, dumbfounded.

It had come from the tower. He stared at it in disbelief. *Had Peace fired upon his own dragon? Impossible!* As long as he rode Ember, no one was supposed to shoot him; that was what made his plan so secure. Deception, shaking his head, angled the dragon upward toward the tower and urged him forward. It had to be a warning; Peace would never be willing to actually fire a lethal shot.

* * *

Justice yelled and cursed. He had missed! The confounded dragon had moved at the last moment and wasted his chance! Justice growled and jerked back the bowstring again. "This time he dies!" he shouted.

* * *

Deception was very close to the tower now; soon Ember would be in range to blast the crossbow and whoever was firing it. But what was this? Peace was not behind the skylance, in fact he was being held back by two soldiers. *What is he...?*

Deception turned to the crossbow and his eyes widened. *Justice! How did he get here?* The reinforcements? Why would Peace have brought *him* out of all people? Deception shook his head. Justice wouldn't fire; it had to be a bluff, a scare tactic. Peace would never let him actually kill Ember.

* * *

Justice locked the string into place and loaded the arrow. He spun the skylance around and aimed it down the approaching dragon's throat. It would be a tighter spot to hit, but Deception was flying straight toward him, giving a clear shot. Justice gripped the lever. This time he would not miss.

* * *

Deception knew that Ember was nearly in range now, but he couldn't shake the feeling of dread. Why was Peace being held off to the side as if by force? If Justice really wasn't going to kill, then why was he aiming directly for them? Deception shook his head. He wouldn't fire. He couldn't!

* * *

Justice gritted his teeth and tightened his grip. "For Highland..." he muttered under his breath.

He fired.

* * *

The only reason Deception survived was because at the very last second, he lost his nerve. Suddenly overcome with panic, he had sent his dragon in a sharp, dangerous plunge, veering left, and the bolt had barely grazed the scales below Ember's wing. Deception felt the dragon shudder as it tried to break its dive, nearly crashing into the tower itself before managing to level out just in time to skim over the grass. Deception pulled him back up for the skies and shook his head in bewilderment.

He had fired! Justice had actually tried to kill Ember! How could Peace have allowed it? Why would he ever have...?

Suddenly, a new and even worse thought entered his mind. What if Justice was now in charge of the mission? What if Peace had no say at all in what happened to his dragon? Deception turned Ember away from the tower and flew out a distance. Suddenly the feeling of immortality his mount had given him began to fade away. He could be killed! Just like a common soldier! It meant nothing to Justice that he rode the Rider's dragon.

He heard two mournful blasts and looked up at the tower to see Justice at the horn. At the tower's base, great double doors were flung open and six skylances were wheeled out. The men were ready, the crossbows already aimed up toward the sky. Several fired and a nearby dragon screeched, tumbling to the ground.

Deception turned his head and saw another dragon brought down by a barrage of arrows fired from the ramparts. Another cry rang out and he turned again just in time to see another beast fall from the sky with a bolt through its heart.

Deception shook his head. *No.... It can't be...*

He looked up to the tower again and saw two riders flying in to take Justice from behind. But right as they swooped in for the kill, Justice spun his crossbow around and fired, spearing one dragon through the heart. Then, without a moment's hesitation, he jumped upon the skylance and leapt from it onto the back of the other dragon as it passed by, killing its rider, and managing to slash its wing with his sword as he leapt back to safety. He landed, crouched and unhurt on the tower as the dragon he injured was sent spiraling and screeching toward the ground.

Deception couldn't believe it. His dragons were being slaughtered!

Peace never would've fired upon the creatures, but with Justice in the tower they seemed to be dropping everywhere. Deception couldn't let this happen to his precious beasts. They were too hard to train. He still needed them! They couldn't all die here!

He desperately tried to get a grip on himself. He had attacked at the wrong time. This was not a good position for him; he needed to retreat and work out a more detailed plan, one not born out of overconfidence. Slowly he raised a horn to his lips—his personal one, formed from an actual dragon's horn—and sounded it three times.

* * *

Justice was taking note of the whole battle. Just as he hoped, the sudden appearance of the skylances, led by Courage, had created widespread panic among the swooping dragons. Several were killed, and the rest seemed to have lost their nerve. Others tried to dive-bomb the crossbows on the ground, but Courage was undaunted by their attacks. He carefully ordered the skylances to fire in turn so that there always remained at least two loaded and ready. Had the dragons attacked at once or with a more decisive strategy, they would've broken through, but their panic kept them from organizing any powerful assaults.

Justice nodded at how things were progressing and looked over to his brother. Peace sat huddled on the floor, his eyes closed and his hands over his ears, as if to block out the screams and cries of the dying creatures he loved so much.

Then came the horn, sounding three times. It must have been the signal for retreat, because immediately the dragons turned away from the city and the attacking army withdrew. Justice slumped to the ground and breathed a sigh of relief. They were leaving! He had done it; he had protected his brother, and the town, and now they were safe!

Well, at least for now. Justice got up and looked toward the fleeing army. It all seemed too easy. Sure, they had taken Deception off guard, but he still had enough of a force to destroy them. Why was he leaving?

Suddenly there were shouts and the sickening sound of beating wings to his right! Justice spun around, drawing his sword, and was just in time to see both of his guards slump to the ground dead as a dragon flew away with his brother in its claws. Justice screamed out a terrible cry of rage and hurled his katana as hard as he could at the fleeing beast, but the blade missed its target and went spinning down to the ground below. Justice cried out in despair and sunk to his knees, watching them fly away.

Of course—now it all made sense. The horn had not been a signal for retreat, but for a backup plan. In the event that Deception could not capture the city, his next move would have logically been to simply target the important people, the few the whole attack was based upon. Even now Justice could hear the wing beats of another dragon approaching behind, no doubt coming for him.

Justice watched in a daze as the dragon carrying his brother headed for the city walls, and he buried his face in his hands. He had failed. He thought back to Peace's letter, how he had promised that nothing would happen to him. But his promise was in vain. His brother had been taken; all was lost.

But then a spark arose within him and anger began to build. *It will not end like this.* He heard the wing beats approaching from behind and mentally began to judge how close the dragon was. *I made a promise.* The dragon was very close now; Justice tensed, his hand moving toward his dagger. *And I never break a promise.*

At the perfect instant he leapt to one side, rebounded off the crossbow, and hurled himself at the dragon's back as it passed over. His dagger was out, but his momentum alone was enough to knock the rider clean off the saddle and straight down from their dizzying height above the city. Justice righted himself in the saddle and picked up the reigns

(Deception, unlike Highland, had all of his dragons fitted with reigns). The beast beneath him seemed confused and twisted its head back to see what had happened. Justice acted quickly, leaping to the side, and slashing the creature's wing.

Instantly the dragon cried out and began losing control, leaning toward its injured side. Justice grabbed the reigns and yanked them the opposite way, forcing the dragon into a more or less level, but painful dive. Up ahead, he saw the dragon with Peace as it neared the city walls.

*No!* Quickly Justice angled his dragon, which was more preoccupied with its pain than where it was being led, downward toward the ground to gain speed, and then upward until it shot above and over the other dragon. Justice jumped, allowing his creature to lose control and plummet to the ground behind him. He braced himself as he fell and angled his body to control his descent, aiming to the right of the dragon beneath him. At the last moment, he straightened out and brought his dagger down across its wing as he fell past.

Justice heard the dragon screech as he continued falling, and then he turned to brace himself as the ground came up with alarming speed. He crashed through the roof of a stable and landed hard on earth covered in hay, which helped to break his fall. He lay there a moment, the wind knocked out of him, and through the gap in the ceiling he saw the dragon lose control and scream as it spiraled to the ground.

"Are you all right, sire?"

Justice looked up and saw Courage staring down at him rather worriedly.

"Yes, I'm fine," he said, but he accepted the general's hand to help him up. Leaning on his shoulder, Justice groaned and limped out of the building. He watched as the dragon he had injured made a crash-landing on the ground, taking the force of the impact in an attempt to protect its rider and prisoner. The moment it was down, the dragon was promptly set upon by scores of soldiers with rope who attempted to wrestle it to

the ground and tie it down until someone was able to stab it through the heart. Its rider was slain and Determination, who led the group of soldiers, was able to pry Peace out of its claw.

Justice limped over to his brother, who seemed to be in a sort of daze. He was rubbing his eyes and looking around at all the dead dragons that dotted the grass.

"I...I..." Peace looked to his brother with pain in his eyes. "Why did you do this? Why did you kill them?"

Justice bristled and barked to some nearby soldiers. "He's fine. Take him back to his tent so that he can recover." Several soldiers helped Peace to his feet and began to escort him away. He struggled against them and continued shouting back.

"They were being forced to serve Deception! They were unhappy; they were prisoners! I could've helped them; I could have saved them! Why? Why did you have to kill them all?"

Justice shook his head and turned away. His brother would be all right; Deception had gotten away, but the city was safe. He had more important things to do.

Suddenly there were cries of alarm and a soldier came running to him.

"The ships! The ships!" he shouted. "They're burning the ships!"

"What!" yelled Justice as he turned and struggled up to the battlements on the wall. Out in the distance, he saw the two ships that had brought them, Peace's and his own, alive in flames. Above them, a dozen dragons circled.

"Why?" asked Courage from behind him. "Why would they burn the ships?"

"So that we can't leave," said Justice in a low voice. "We're trapped in Deception's own country now; he can take his time planning his next attack. I fear that few will escape this place with their lives."

* * *

Deception flew with his forces away from the city of Hope, contemplating his recent defeat. Things hadn't gone as badly as they could have. Sure, he had lost dragons, but he and Ember were still alive—that was what mattered. He had failed to capture either Peace or Justice, but most of their army was wounded, so they would not prove to be a very powerful force outside those walls.

But even with these thoughts, Deception could not rest at ease, for he saw a way his plan might fail. As long as there had only been Peace, he had been certain of victory. Peace would not risk killing his own dragon, so Deception knew he was safe. But now Justice, the great and feared general with no weaknesses, was here and willing to pay any price to see him dead...

Deception shuttered. He could still do it, but now he had to be careful; he had to keep Ember and the other dragons away from that accursed man. Yes, he had welcomed the challenge, but this he had not planned for. He turned his face forward, the words of Peace playing through his mind.

*Be careful what you wish for...*

5

# In the Darkened Heights

After finding the throne room vacant, Ruthless eventually located Deception in the dungeons. He was standing in front of an iron-bound window, watching Ember being tortured in a large room below. The stone walls shook with the dragon's cries as the men continued to sear its skin with hot iron and lash its wings with whips. Deception looked down upon the scene calmly, in a satisfied manner, a small object in his hand. Ruthless looked back and forth between dragon and master before speaking.

"Is it because of our failure that you do this to him?"

Deception smiled slightly but did not look away. "I suppose you could view it that way. In truth though, I've been doing this ever since he was first brought here; it's a procedure that we go through regularly." Ruthless remained silent for several moments, hoping that Deception would elaborate. Eventually he did.

"It's called fear conditioning," he said, holding out the object in his hand. It appeared to be a small, red horn, about the size of a whistle. "I blow this, and then the torture starts. The dragon will eventually begin to associate the pain with the sound, and then fear the horn itself. I do this with all of my dragons, although with Ember especially."

"But what benefit does that serve?" asked Ruthless.

"It's power!" Deception exclaimed, throwing his arms out. "It gives me a control over them unlike anything else. If a dragon turns on me, then all I have to do is blow this to send it cowering in fear."

"But why Ember? With the Curse's enchantment, you have no need to fear where his loyalties lie."

"True," said Deception with a smile. "But as long as the Curse binds his soul to me, why should I not take the opportunity to bind him in every other way possible? He is mine! I will not lose him! He will never be taken from me!"

"But you still fear he might be? Is that why you summoned me?"

Deception was silent; his smile faded.

"Yes."

"But you have no need to worry. The Curse keeps him—"

"I do not fear Peace's attempts to reclaim him; I fear the attempts to kill him!"

"But he is safe here."

"No! Justice lives, and as long as he remains alive, we are in danger."

"There is nothing Justice can do. His army is in shambles, and this stronghold is one of the most fortified in the country. Besides all of that, if he tries to come here his way is blocked by the great river to the south which flows right out into the sea; without his ships—"

"I need him dead!" shouted Deception—to Ruthless his face seemed desperate. "I care not what obstacles he faces; he will find a way, he always has. I need him dead!"

Ruthless smiled. He liked his master being dependent on him. "You need him killed? That happens to be my specialty."

"I know; that is why I called you here. In a few days, he will have reached the southern bank of the great river. I need you to meet him there and destroy him. I want Peace alive but destroy everyone else. Take all the men you want—anything you need is at your disposal, just kill Justice!"

"Of course, my lord. It will be easy; I could decimate what's left of his forces with only a hundred men."

"Then take a thousand! Do not underestimate him; he must be destroyed!" Deception leaned close to his general. "This is the height of my triumph; everything I have is at stake! Go swiftly; if you succeed, then you will be made second-in-command. You will answer only to me, and when I take Tarenthia you will be made steward over all the Shadowlands. They will be yours to rule as you please—just get rid of that accursed man!"

Ruthless nodded, hoping that the glee he felt within did not shine in his eyes. His master was far more desperate than he had ever hoped.

He smiled. "It will be done, my lord."

* * *

It was not long after the attack that Justice prepared his men to move out. He sensed they were running out of time. While the city of Hope was certainly a defensible position, he knew that with a little more planning and a little less recklessness, Deception could conquer it easily. Therefore, their only option was to move out and try to find their enemy before he could finish recovering from his defeat. If there was a chance that they might catch him unawares and stop him, then maybe there was a chance that they would all survive. It was very unlikely, but Justice saw no other option.

Peace traveled quietly on horseback alongside his brother. The large number of injured soldiers slowed them greatly, as did the six bulky skylances that Justice had insisted they bring with them. Most of the city's inhabitants were traveling with them as well, and it was not hard to see why—with the Dragon Rider out of the city, there was a good possibility that Deception would choose not to harass the town of Hope anymore but there was no means of being sure. Justice had given all of the town's citizens the option of coming along with him under his protection.

Peace smiled rather sadly at their long caravan of weary soldiers, injured men, and frightened children. He did not resent his brother's decision to invite so many along (he could be caring and protective of the innocent, despite his hard and calculating nature), but at the same time Peace wondered if their party was not under greater danger being such a large, slow-moving target. Justice claimed that the skylances would protect them from dragon air-raids but what they all feared was a land army, their own force only possessing about two hundred men that could still wield a sword and more than three times that many who could not. There were very few who had received no wounds.

For the first two days of traveling, Peace said very little, and his brother traveled in equal silence. On the third day however, as the sun was beginning its decent in the western sky, he rode up alongside Justice and made an apology.

"I'm sorry, my brother, for the way that I acted. You defended us, went to great length to rescue me, and in return I only became angry with you. I'm sorry for my reaction to the slain dragons."

Beside him his brother nodded. "I understand, and I bear no ill will."

They continued to ride in silence for a while, and Justice came close to apologizing himself for having so many of the dragons slaughtered. He knew of his brother's special attachment to the creatures and perhaps he could have let Peace tame some of the grounded ones—they definitely would have been useful to have along now—but Justice couldn't quite bring himself to say it. He had done what needed to be done, and that was that. He did however realize, as they continued to ride along in silence, that his lack of any comment would likely cause his brother to think that he didn't care at all, so he attempted to start a conversation.

"If you were able to convert the dragon at the gatehouse, then why do you think you are having such problems with Ember? Twice now you have tried."

"I don't know," said Peace sadly. "He just felt...different. He doesn't respond to me anymore."

Justice remembered the King's words: *There may be more to this than you realize.*

"I wonder," he said at last, "since he is the Rider's dragon, if Deception didn't take some extra precautions with Ember—you did say he told you on the beach that he had left him with some type of safeguard?"

"Yes, that's what he said—and when I tried to reach Ember the second time, it felt almost as if there were some type of barrier—I think Deception mentioned a curse of some sort."

"Really? A curse? Do you suppose he is using some type of enchantment?"

"Perhaps..." said Peace, and then his face brightened. "Of course; maybe he is! Maybe that's why Ember's resisting me. If there's a curse, then maybe he hasn't actually forsaken me! I could still get him to come back!"

Justice turned to Courage, who was riding beside him. "Quickly— question the citizens with us and see if you can find anyone who would know about any enchantments Deception might have in this land."

"Yes, sire," said the general and immediately turned his horse around to inquire amongst the people behind them.

Peace turned to his brother. "You're helping me? I thought that you didn't care about reclaiming Ember."

"I care about finding Deception, and if I must kill Ember to do so, I will. But I would prefer not, if possible, especially knowing how much he means to you. If this is something that can be easily fixed, then I would be more than happy to see the two of you reunited."

"But didn't you say that Ember has to die, because of his treason?" asked Peace, daring to hope.

"If he has fought against our kingdom willingly, then yes, he does. But if an enchantment forced him to, then he may yet escape with his life. Either way, however, you would still have some time with him before we sail home. You would at least have a chance to say farewell."

Peace nodded. He desperately hoped that all of their troubles were just because of a curse, that it would be something easy to break. Maybe, just maybe, he could still get Ember back home alive.

* * *

They rode on for several more hours until Courage returned with the librarian of Hope. He was short, even on horseback, and he squinted to see anything that wasn't directly in front of his eyes. But he had studied books all his life and appeared very knowledgeable.

"A curse you say? I don't suppose you mean *the* Curse. I heard rumors that Deception had found it, although I'd hoped they weren't true. I had no idea he would've applied it to Ember, or I would've told you before he attacked the first time."

"What exactly is the Curse?" asked Justice. "Why have I never heard it mentioned before during my education in Highland?"

The librarian settled back in his saddle as if he was about to tell a long tale. "The Curse is a remnant of the past age," he said. "Long ago, before Highland came to power and when all dragons were still untamed and free, there were many nations that had struggled to rise up and rule over each other. Of course, many saw the dragons as the key—whoever could control them could control everyone else. Unfortunately, the drag-ons proved impossible to break. The nations tried everything they could think of; they tried taming them like other animals, they tried bargaining with them, reasoning with them, forcing them, but nothing worked and eventually they turned to magic. The Curses were devised."

"Curses?" asked Peace. "Are there more than one?"

"There used to be, but not anymore."

"How did they work?" asked Justice.

"Each Curse was an enchantment placed upon a particular object, such as a stone or medallion. They could be linked telepathically to one human and one dragon at a time; the human would send commands to the Curse, and the Curse would force the dragon to obey. Using this technique, the nations were able to use the dragons against each other."

"Didn't the dragons try to resist the Curse?" asked Peace with concern.

"No, they didn't; that was the point. The Curse only worked because it caused the dragons to stop caring what happened to them, mostly through turning their attention and ambition to a strange hunger it created inside of them. The odd thing was that the dragons couldn't actually figure out what the hunger was for; they would focus so hard on the longing itself, and on a strange pleasure derived from it, that they were never able to identify what it was, though it drove them mad."

"A hunger?" asked Justice.

"Yes, a hunger. In fact, that is how Deception is controlling most of his dragons. There is only one Curse now, and so he needs an alternate method for the rest. Because he can impart emotions to any dragon he touches, he simply gives them the hunger inspired by the Curse and it affects them the same way that Curse would, although without any actual enchantment, the effect is temporary, and risks being broken by another person."

"Deception can cause a dragon to feel anything he wants just by touching it?" asked Peace with surprise, "How did he come to have this ability?"

"Anyone can learn to do it," said the librarian. "Haven't you ever had your emotions manipulated slightly through touch? Dragons that are broken and tamed according to Highland's methods are incredibly susceptible to it."

Peace looked forward, shaking his head. "Why?" he whispered. "Why was I never told? I could have prevented all of this from happening. Why did no one ever tell me of my own dragon's weakness?"

"Because you were the Rider," said Justice.

"You knew?"

"Yes, but only because the King told me before I left. It's a carefully guarded secret."

"Why? Why wouldn't I be told something so powerful about my own dragon?"

"Because it had the potential to destroy your relationship," said Justice sharply. "Think about it. If during your years with him you knew that at any moment you could give Ember any feeling or emotion you wanted, wouldn't you have, say, given him joy all of the time?"

"Yes, I would have."

"That is why you were never told. If Ember learned that he could receive any feeling he wanted directly from you, he would begin to follow you only to experience those feelings. The love between the two of you would have deteriorated into nearly what Deception has done with the Curse: a relationship based purely off mutual gain. Feelings should not be under such direct control; it is unfortunate that we cannot change the way our dragons are trained."

They rode on in silence for a few moments. Then Justice turned to the librarian.

"I'm sorry, but I appear to have interrupted your story. Can you tell why the people of old ceased using the Curses? It seems like they were an effective weapon."

"Yes, they were," said the librarian. "But the nations encountered two problems that hindered their efforts. The first was that any dragon ensnared by a Curse only lived for a few weeks, the ravenous hunger apparently destroyed their minds."

"What! They *died*?" cried Peace. He desperately tried to guess how long Ember had been under Deception's power.

"Yes, I'm afraid they did. To the nations however, that was only an inconvenience because it meant they had to find new dragons. The real problem they encountered was Highland.

"While the nations had been busy fighting and trying to control the dragons, Highland, which had not engaged in any of the fights, had developed a new way of taming them. By submerging a dragon egg in cold water, they were able to get the hatchling inside to become more docile, dependent, and ultimately tamable. Then, instead of trying to control them with magic, the people of Highland developed the Links and used them to create relationships between themselves and their broken dragons.

Of course, it took a while as taming dragons with this method had to be done with newborn hatchlings instead of full-grown dragons, but eventually their bond proved stronger than the bond of the Curse, and Highland was able to conquer the other nations. They outlawed all enchantments aside from the Links and had every Curse destroyed. One however, was fabled to have been brought here and hidden. It was a search for it that brought your father here years ago, and after he failed to find it, a search that brought Deception shortly thereafter. It appears now that he has succeeded in locating it and has applied it to Ember."

"Is there any way of breaking the Curse?" asked Peace desperately. "If we were to destroy the object the Curse is connected to, would Ember be released?"

"Supposedly yes," said the librarian slowly, "but it is likely that Ember would not remember you or anything else before his enchantment."

"Where would this Curse be?" asked Justice. "Where could we find it?"

"It would likely be with Deception or Ember, as it needs to be close to the dragon to have full effect."

Justice shook his head. "I'm sorry Peace, but this doesn't seem like it will be possible to break. Deception will no doubt have the Curse well hidden, and what benefit would it be to us if we can only change Ember from being a dragon that hates you to one that doesn't remember you?"

Peace faltered. "No, he will remember me, I'm sure. We have to try."

"It's too risky; Deception will guard that Curse with his life. If it was something simple to break, then I gladly would do so. But as things are, your dragon shelters the enemy; we have no other option."

Peace shook his head, desperately trying to fight the despair that clouded his mind. "No...no...let's not focus on killing Ember; let's just focus on Deception. That's what you wanted anyway, and we can decide on what to do with Ember after that. And besides, strategically speaking, wouldn't it be easier to kill a man rather than a dragon?"

"Unless the man is *riding* the dragon," said Justice grimly.

"I'm sorry," said the librarian, whose head had been turning back and forth between them, "I'm terribly sorry, but I'm afraid that what you are suggesting will not accomplish what you desire. Killing Deception, who is the commander of the Curse, will necessarily kill Ember, the receiver."

"What!" exclaimed Peace. He looked to his brother beseechingly and then wished he hadn't.

"Don't start trying to convince me not to kill Deception too," said Justice gravely. "That man is too dangerous to us and to Highland for me to simply walk away."

"But, but—" said Peace desperately. For so long he had held onto the hope that Ember could be redeemed; for so long he had been seeking to forgive him, to accept him back again. It had been his motivation, his driving force. He couldn't possibly give up now.

Justice shook his head sadly. "I'm sorry," he said. "I really am. I wanted to reclaim him if possible, but..." he sighed.

"Peace, Ember is living in sickness, a sickness that's killing him. Even if we could break the Curse, it would only leave him lost and alone, devoid of everything he knows. You are his Rider; you're supposed to do what is best for him. Would it not be kinder, would it not be a *mercy*, to kill him and put him out of his misery? That is the best we can do for him now; and if he will die anyway for his treason, then would it not be better for him to do so now, while he rages against us, than to be released just long enough to taste a freedom he will not be allowed to live out?"

Peace shook his head desperately. "I can't do it," he moaned. "I know that dragon—I loved him. Even if he were to lose his memory, I would still want to give him another chance. I can't possible kill him."

Justice placed a hand on his brother's shoulder sympathetically. "Peace, I'm sorry, but your dragon is already dead. There is nothing left of him now except what Deception has made him to be. Concentrate on the man; if you cannot kill Ember then kill the one who destroyed him. At least then he will be avenged."

Peace shook his brother's hand off and stared blindly ahead, saying nothing. He couldn't give up, even if everyone else had. But yet Justice seemed to be right; perhaps the kindest thing he could do now was to kill Ember. Peace shook his head. He couldn't believe it. He didn't want to believe it.

* * *

It was near evening when they came to the river. The weary troop of people had reached near exhaustion, so Justice sent men to scout for a good place to make camp along the shore. They soon decided on a large flat plain resting in the shadow of a great cliff. The vertical wall would protect them from any attacks behind, and with the great river about half a mile before them it seemed like a relatively secure position. Justice was slightly concerned that their enemy could sneak to the top of the cliff and rain boulders and arrows down upon them, but their company was too tired to go much farther and the injured needed to be treated, so Justice let them rest. Of the two griffins Peace had brought, one had recovered enough to fly so Justice sent it out to scout around, hoping that the night would be quiet and calm for the people to get some much-needed sleep.

He stayed up long into the night, watching the river and gathering information about their surroundings. In the end, he had to summon the librarian again as he seemed to know the most about lands outside the city of Hope.

"That river before us is one of the greatest in the entire land, and possibly in Tarenthia as well," he said. "Beyond it lays the city of Despair, which appears to be Deception's current base, from what I have gathered."

"Can it be taken easily?" asked Justice. "Will there be dragons defending it?"

"I don't know much about the dragons," said the librarian, "except that they seem to be more populous in the north. If Deception has any, it will be because he brought them down south. The city itself however does not need dragons for protection; it is one of the most fortified, well-stocked castles in all Shadowlands. I don't see how it will be possible for us to overtake."

"Then let's concentrate on one problem at a time," said Justice. "First we need to get past the river; is there any way around?"

"Not for several hundred miles. If you follow the river west, it only becomes wider and deeper until it enters the sea. If you follow it east, you will have to travel nearly to the other coast before finding a way around; it almost splits the whole land in half."

"Are there no bridges or crossings?"

"None; the river is far too wide for that; the only way across requires ships, which Deception seemed very careful to destroy."

"So, we traveled all of this way to get stuck? Is there nothing we can do?"

"Not that I can think of," said the librarian sadly. "Perhaps there is—."

"Sire!" yelled Determination, running toward them. "Sire, there's an attack coming! An enormous vessel has been spotted halfway across the river; it carries near a thousand men!"

Justice jumped up quickly. "Hurry then; prepare our soldiers!"

"Wait!" shouted the librarian also jumping up. "What was the symbol upon the sail?"

"It bore the image of a roaring dragon with a sword protruding from its chest," said Determination.

The librarian stumbled back several steps, shaking his head. "Oh, no; this cannot be."

"What is it?" asked Justice firmly.

"It's Ruthless; the most feared, most cunning general under Deception's command! He's come to destroy us; we will all be killed!"

"I do not fear him!" barked Justice. "I have faced many terrible battles, but I have survived. There's always a weakness, always a way through."

"Justice, you don't understand. What you are to Tarenthia, that man is to us here. He is unstoppable, unbeatable."

"Well, he hasn't met me," said Justice sharply, before turning back to the camp.

"What are we going to do?" asked Determination. "We have to stop him, but I don't see how; our men are too few and there are the wounded to think of."

"Then if we cannot overcome him, we must outsmart him."

They found Peace amongst the tents and Justice quickly explained the situation. "I need a plan," he said. "You were always good at this sort of thing; help me figure out what to do."

"I don't know," said Peace, rather startled. "I was never a general like you; I've never faced a situation like this before."

"But you traveled throughout all of Tarenthia; surely you must've encountered seemingly impossible scenarios."

"Perhaps, but Ember was always with me."

"Think; you can do it! You'll come up with something clever, like what you did at Watergate."

Peace shook his head sadly. "I don't think I can. Deception has outsmarted me since then; I certainly didn't predict his plan at World's End."

Justice looked at him, his eyes suddenly wide. "Yes, of course! You're a genius! It's so simple!"

"What? What did I say?" asked Peace, bewildered.

"It's not what you just said, it's something you said before." Justice looked up toward the steep cliffs at the back of the camp and then turned to Determination.

"How fast can we move the wounded?"

* * *

Ruthless watched as his men filed out from the ship and formed ranks upon the sand. There was the camp laid out ahead of them, quiet, quaint, and peaceful with small fires burning in the dusk. Ruthless smiled in anticipation. Their peace would not last much longer. He rubbed his hands in the chilly air and advanced to the head of his army. He had taken about eight hundred men—he could not dream of needing the full thousand; all they would need to do is charge, take the camp unawares, and then he would be named second-in-command.

"Shall we start the attack?" asked one of the rank leaders.

Ruthless held up a hand to wait. He wanted to charge ahead and into the camp as much as his men, but he hadn't gotten as far as he had by being reckless. Something nagged inside of him. It seemed odd how unprotected the tents were. Sure, the cliff provided some security, but it could still be easily approached and surrounded from three sides.

But then Ruthless shook his head. No, it was probably nothing; Justice had simply needed to make camp somewhere quickly before nightfall because of the many wounded he carried—that prevented him from looking for a better spot. Even now, they likely were all asleep; they probably never even saw his ship. They would be caught completely unawares.

* * *

Justice hid with his men behind their cover and peeked out at the approaching army away in the distance.

"This plan is not going to work," said the librarian beside him.

"Be patient, he'll take the bait," said Justice.

"Do you really think he will fall for it?" asked Peace. "He is a renowned general."

"He will," said Justice. "He has to."

"It looks as if they're about to invade the camp," said Determination beside him.

The librarian shook his head and huddled next to them. "This is not going to work," he mumbled.

* * *

Ruthless was unsure. His men stood ready to charge, but something just didn't feel right. The camp seemed just a little too quiet, too calm. *Wouldn't Justice have put up more guards?*

He shook his head. No, the man had probably set up camp too quickly. He probably wasn't expecting any attack. Still the doubts within him would not be quelled. Ruthless paced the ground restlessly. Part of him kept saying to start the invasion, but the deeper, more experienced part of him held back. It was his sharp instinct, an asset that had always warned him of any tricks being played. Again and again that honed instinct had saved him, and now it was uneasy.

*Come on Justice, you've got to be smarter than this.* He nearly gave the signal again to attack, but he just couldn't; Deception's warning kept playing over in his mind.

*Do not underestimate him...*

Ruthless grunted and grabbed a spyglass. He peered through the scope at the quiet, innocent camp, looking for guards, people, anything. He saw some soldiers standing at attention, spears in hand. He took a closer look. The soldiers were standing stiff and straight; they didn't look quite right. Ruthless grinned slowly and lowered the spyglass.

Fake! They were mock soldiers, stuffed with straw to give the impression of a guard. Ruthless looked up at the cliffs and scanned them with the telescope. It didn't seem like—There! Smoke! He grinned wildly. Of course, it was the perfect plan; create a decoy camp and assemble the soldiers above it. When the invasion started, they could simply rain down arrows and boulders upon his army, maybe even start an avalanche. Ruthless let out a sigh of relief and the instinct inside of him relaxed. *I've got you now, Justice.*

He turned to his men. "Don't attack! Station three hundred here and send the others off a few at a time, quietly and stealthily. Send them around to the other side of the cliff where it's not as steep to steal up behind them."

He smiled. He didn't even have to go. He would stay down on the shore and watch it all—watch as Justice was outwitted and then killed. He had won!

* * *

Down at the base of the cliff, in the quiet, peaceful little camp with its straw guardsmen, there was concealed Justice's army, along with the injured, the citizens, and all the others; each of them hiding quietly in the tents to give the impression that the base was deserted. Justice crouched behind the furthermost tents, with Peace and Determination at his side. Huddled close to the seemingly abandoned fire sat the librarian.

"Why aren't they attacking?" whispered the librarian anxiously. "We're right here out in the open!"

"That's the point," said Peace. "It's too easy."

Justice smiled. "You suspected Deception of risking everything on a bluff before, my brother; that's what I remembered. Given our situation, I really couldn't think of much else."

"Sire!" cried Determination quietly. "I think they saw the smoke on the cliffs; some of them are leaving."

"Smoke?" asked the librarian.

"Yes," said Peace. "Justice has a man up on the cliffs starting small fires. Ruthless will no doubt expect that to be our real camp and go attack."

"But won't the man be killed when the soldiers come?"

Peace sighed and looked forward. "Possibly; we needed a man with great bravery. That is why we sent Courage. He has the griffin though, so he should be able to escape."

"Sire," said Determination. "They've taken the bait! The soldiers are leaving!"

Justice spun to face him; his eye alive with fiery excitement. "They're going? How much of the army? How many stayed to guard the ship?"

"It's hard to tell, but it seems that there are about three hundred. We number less, but we have the advantage of surprise; I think that we can take them!"

Justice smiled.

"Let's hope those wounded can be moved as quickly as you said they could."

* * *

From atop the cliff, Courage peeked down upon the tranquil night and the sleepy camp below. He huddled next to one of the many small fires he had made and shivered in the cold. To his side the griffin stood restlessly, preening the feathers on its wing and waiting for the battle to start. Courage also waited; his job was finished but if he left now the men on the shore would see the two of them and the plan would be ruined. He would have to wait—wait until Ruthless' men clambered up the cliff and were too far away to help their comrades. Only then could Justice start the attack.

Courage got up from the fire and paced restlessly. It had been over an hour since the majority of Ruthless' forces had left the shore. How close were they? Were they climbing up the cliff right at that moment? Would men suddenly appear all around him? He shivered against the brisk wind. What was taking Justice so long? How long was he planning on waiting before—?

There! A battle cry! Quickly, Courage dashed to the edge of the cliff and looked down upon the camp. Justice had charged! He was leading his men in a full sprint to the guard party on the shore, the wounded and injured being pulled along right behind them in horse-drawn supply carts. Before the soldiers guarding the ship had a chance to realize what was happening, Justice would be upon them and fighting with the skill and speed he was known for. Courage sat back against his griffin. He would watch from up here a while; he loved to see his commander at work.

* * *

Ruthless was dumbfounded. All in one moment the peace of the night had been shattered by a great war cry followed by the noise of hundreds of charging men and horses. The general leapt up from the ground and ran to the front of the camp; his eyes widened in astonishment. Immediately he realized all that had happened, that he had been tricked, that the men he had sent would now be too far away to help, that the ship he brought was about to be stolen.

He shook his head, trying to bring himself to his senses. He could still do it—he had at least as many men; they could break the charge!

"All men, to arms!" he hollered. "Archers assemble in the front; move the ship away from the shore!"

Around him men scrambled to their feet, trying to find their weapons and get in line. The army was just moments away!

Ruthless rushed to the center of his forces and drew his sword. "Archers, assemble!" he called out. They formed lines out in front; behind them, the swordsmen struggled to get into ranks.

"Take aim!"

The archers drew back their bows. The enemy force was almost upon them!

"Fire!"

* * *

In one moment, Justice lost nearly fifty of his men as those heading the charge were hit by a barrage of arrows and stumbled. He rushed ahead; his katana held high. He could see the archers ahead of him, reloading their weapons. At his side, Determination shouted, and the men behind did the same. The archers drew back their bows again, but then with a shout and a mighty leap Justice plunged into their ranks. Few of the arrows hit their targets as his men shattered the line of bowmen and burst into the brunt of the forces behind.

Instantly, the battle became a cacophony of cries, shouts, and clanging swords. Justice fought with a fury he did not know he had, and around him men fell to his blade. At first he feared that his men would be swallowed by the larger force, but soon it became clear that their surprise attack had left the enemy too startled and shaken to put up a proper resistance. All around him Justice saw his men fighting and shouting with amazing courage and ferocity that seemed to overcome anyone who stood in their way.

He looked forward, and as he struggled his way through the dense forest of soldiers he hollered out, "To the ship! Do not let it get away!"

Then suddenly he had no time to shout anything more as he was engaged by Ruthless himself! The general was by far the most experienced swordsman Justice had ever met, and for a moment he felt he might be overwhelmed. Then suddenly Determination was at his side slashing wildly to give his commander a chance to get his bearings.

"Don't worry about me!" hollered Justice. "Just take the ship!"

Quickly drawing his dagger along with his sword, Justice lunged toward Ruthless and gave Determination a chance to escape. The enemy commander grunted and fought for all he was worth. He struck with great speed and strength, clutching his sword in both hands.

Justice was forced to rely on his agility and reflexes as he dodged or deflected most of the blows. His adversary seemed unstoppable! Time and time again, Justice was forced to jump back as the fighting continued all around them. He fumed with frustration and anger.

Up ahead of him, Determination finally broke through to the shore—but the ship was already a way out in the water. He refused to be stopped however, and with hardly a second thought, he leapt into the icy river and began to swim with all his might for the vessel ahead. Behind him, several men followed his lead and the sound of splashes rippled through the air.

* * *

Up upon the cliff, Courage watched as the two armies battled, now completely intermixed with each other, making it hard to tell in the dusk who was winning.

"Explain the meaning of this!"

Courage jolted to his feet and spun around just in time to see a man pointing a sword at him. A host of soldiers stood behind.

"What is going on! Where are Justice and his men?"

Courage smiled faintly. "You've been beaten," he said. "You've been outwitted."

The man snarled in rage and swung his sword at him. Courage ducked and ran to where his griffin perched a few feet away. Quickly, he leapt onto its back as the creature spread its wings and prepared to fly.

"Bring him down!" came a cry from behind as the griffin lifted off the ground, beating its wings powerfully. Then Courage heard the sickening whistle of arrows piercing the griffin's feathers. The poor beast cried out, tried to hold its course, and then tumbled fluttering to the ground, landing hard.

Soldiers quickly surrounded them. Shakily, Courage dismounted his downed beast and looked into its eyes, full of sadness and pain. He rubbed the creature's feathery neck. "It's all right," he whispered. "You tried your best; I am not ashamed of you."

"What is going on!" cried out the captain again.

"You lost," Courage said simply without turning. He gently rubbed his forehead against the griffin's and then gestured out toward the battle on the shore far below. Justice had apparently broken through because men stood at the water's edge and in the waning evening light there could be seen the ripples of soldiers swimming out for the ship. They had almost reached it.

Courage viewed the battle for a few moments and then turned back, content. Beside him, the griffin gave a fearful moan.

"You will die for this!" cried the captain. Courage smiled; his eyes soft. He placed his hand on the beast beside him and drew his sword.

"If I die," he said, "then I die for my King, for the Dragon Rider, for Justice, and for my comrade." He was unafraid, unshaken.

With a cry the captain charged, his men closing in, and Courage wielded his sword for the last time.

* * *

Justice seethed as his assailant continued to fight with a speed and viciousness unlike any he had ever seen. Justice moved like lightning, spinning to create a deadly circle of steel around himself and then blocking and slashing with first one weapon and then the other. But to his shock he found that his opponent was still more than his equal, and that as they dueled neither could gain any ground. Justice was enraged. His sword and dagger, with which he could take on five soldiers at once, were proving inadequate to overcome just this one man!

He lashed out in frustration and made a dangerous lunge for his opponent's throat, but Ruthless was swifter and ducked, swinging out with his own blade and causing Justice to stumble as he leapt backward. His defenses faltered and Ruthless laughed wildly, bringing his blade back for a final swing. But then suddenly it was blocked by another sword.

"Peace!" cried Justice, desperately struggling to his feet as the enemy general turned to his brother, attacking wildly. Justice came to his aid and for just a moment the two of them fought side by side as Ruthless spun and blocked with amazing speed, rhythmically countering first one and then the other. Then suddenly, a well-placed kick knocked Justice flat on his back and his brother faltered, losing his footing.

"No! Peace!" cried Justice desperately, rising to one knee and hurling his dagger. Ruthless turned briefly at the shout and the dagger struck squarely in his chest. He froze for a moment with the impact, and then his weapon fell from his hand and his body collapsed on the ground. Peace timidly rose.

Justice got to his feet and stabbed his sword into the ground angrily. "What do you think you were doing?" he shouted. "You could have been killed!"

His brother shrugged. "I thought you needed help."

Justice heaved an angry sigh but said nothing as he retrieved his weapons and moved toward the riverbank. All around him the fighting grew quieter and quieter until it stopped altogether. Justice looked and saw that his men had won, but just barely. Many had fallen and those who had escaped injury before were now struggling simply to stand.

Justice turned to face the river. "Did we capture the ship?" he asked.

"Determination swam out to it. I saw him climb up the anchor chain with several of his men."

"Did he take it?"

"I don't know. I guess we will find out soon."

Several minutes passed, but Justice did not lose hope. Determination had never failed him before. Then slowly, ever so slowly, the ship turned and began to sail back toward the beach. Justice smiled and his men cheered.

"Hurry!" he said to Peace. "Let's get everyone on board before those men on the cliff return!"

* * *

Several hours later, Justice stood with his soldiers on deck with nothing but glistening water all around. It was the first time, perhaps since they had arrived in the Shadowlands, that he felt they were relatively safe. Sure, there were always dragons to consider, but the skylances had been brought aboard and Deception would likely not hear about their victory and Ruthless's defeat until tomorrow. They had made it.

Many of them.

For a moment, Justice felt his joy replaced by anger, anger for how many soldiers had given their lives fighting for him, anger for his lost general that had always stood steadfast and undoubting. Justice fumed. Courage had always reminded him of Peace; he was brave, clever, and even compassionate toward the beasts. Now he was gone; his life ripped away by one of Deception's men.

He sensed Determination approaching him from the side. He knew what he was about to ask but let him do so anyway.

"What will we do now? We have a ship; should we sail to the river's mouth and head home?"

Justice stared out into the distance. Too many people had died, had been sacrificed. He could not let them die in vain.

"No. Deception will pay for what he has done."

Beside him, Determination smiled.

"I was hoping you would say that."

# 6

# Beware the Place that Lightning Strikes

Deception paced the throne room fuming—his steps angry, his mind racing. Ruthless had failed! He had taken near a thousand men, but now Justice approached in his very ship! The man was a nightmare; he couldn't be stopped!

Deception seethed; his fists shook at the air. Justice was coming. He was coming for him! Of course it seemed impossible—it seemed unthinkable—that he could serve any threat, that he could overcome the second-most fortified castle in the land. But yet, he had defeated Ruthless.

Deception shook his head. No, there were over two thousand men stationed here, the walls were high and thick; that phantom couldn't possibly break them down. He would be a fool to fight; what could he possibly do?

For just a second, Deception stopped to allow a happy thought to enter his mind. Maybe Justice didn't know what he was up against.

Maybe he would be taken off guard. Maybe he would even be killed while fighting!

Deception shook off his smile and continued his pacing. He didn't come as far as he had by underestimating his enemy. Best-case scenario: Justice would be killed. Worst-case scenario: that man would somehow, miraculously, find some way to overcome all his men, all his defenses, and be little more than stalled by his efforts.

Deception growled at the air. It wasn't enough; it wasn't enough! As long as the Dragon Rider Pact stood, Justice would not hesitate to kill Ember. Peace could simply find a new dragon and still become king. Peace had to be the one that died—then Ember's life would need to be preserved long enough for him to receive a new Rider. But Peace couldn't be killed as long as his brother protected him!

Deception ranted and pulled at his hair. He tried to get a grip on himself. If he could kill Peace then all would be put right, and in order to kill Peace he would have to be separated from his brother, just as he had been separated from Ember. Deception beat his head. Think! He had done it before, how could he do it again? What were they most likely to disagree on? What could he use to separate them?

Deception's head snapped up, his eyes widening. Of course! It was so simple! He breathed a sigh of relief, allowing himself to relax again. It was all right; it would work. He could still do it. He smiled.

*Come on Justice; do the impossible again—it still won't stop me.*

* * *

Peace watched as the men set up camp on the shore. Ahead of them stood Deception's castle, or at least one of them anyway. He was in control of nearly the whole country, so no doubt he had more. To the side, Peace saw his brother ordering his men to pitch the tents and set up places to shelter the wounded. He smiled sadly. There were so many wounded. Yes, Justice had taken the ship, but it had cost him much. Nearly everyone was injured now, many quite badly. There were only about fifty who could hold a sword, and even those not well. The whole force reminded him of a wave that had once roared proudly through the sea, broken forcefully upon the land, and now barely had the momentum to touch the rock it had been set on washing away. The expedition was burned out; it had fought and fallen and now struggled just to stand before the greatest challenge of all. Peace shook his head and wandered back to his tent. He didn't even know what he planned on doing when he found Ember. That is, if Justice didn't find him first.

That night, Peace dreamed.

*He dreamed that things were as they were before, when he had ridden Ember through the plains of Tarenthia. He felt the wind rush against them as they flew, trees passing like a blur below them. Peace leaned back against his dragon's back and smiled warmly up at the sky.*

*"Shall we head to the East?" he felt Ember ask. "I heard that two kingdoms are in a dispute and may soon go to war. It could be fun."*

*Peace laughed. "I think I've had enough adventure for a long while."*

*Ahead of him, he felt Ember snort in agreement. "Yes, I think you are right. There will always be time later. We could just fly for today; we haven't done that for a long time."*

*"Yes, let's. It is good to be flying again, my Eldar."*

*"My Eldar," Ember agreed.*

*And so the two of them simply flew. They flew over lakes and coves, pines and forests, plains and mountains. Forever it seemed they flew, just the two of them with no distractions or interruptions. Then, as the sun faded and evening set in, Ember landed on a wide plateau and folded his wings.*

*"Why did we land here?" asked Peace, sitting up. And then his eyes widened in horror when he saw the man. About thirty feet away Deception stood, saber drawn. He waited silently without approaching.*

*"Why are we here?" asked Peace again, sliding down Ember's back to land at his side. The dragon turned his head to look at him, his eyes sad.*

*"He has to be overcome eventually, my Rider. I've tried to fight him for so long, but I could not. I've tried to fly away but my wings always bring me back here. I need you to set me free from him. I need you to fight."*

*Peace rubbed his head gently against the dragon's scaly neck. "Can't you leave?"*

*"I cannot. I'm sorry."*

*"I don't think that I can overcome him."*

*"I believe in you. You are my Rider; fight for me."*

*Peace slowly left his dragon's side and advanced forward. The figure of Deception moved toward him with equal speed. Peace drew his sword, eyeing his enemy. He felt afraid.*

*Briefly, he turned back toward Ember. "You will wait for me?"*

*"Yes, my Eldar. Though I be imprisoned in the deepest of dungeons, I will always wait for you. You have my love. Never forget that; I have always loved you, and I always will. Free me from him."*

*Peace turned forward and saw that Deception was now directly in front of him. He raised his saber to strike, and Peace held up his sword to block the blow.*

The clang of steel startled Peace from his sleep. He sat up, listening, and heard it again—the sound of someone hammering on a tent peg with a hammer. He let himself fall back down again with a heavy sigh. Something moved at his feet; he looked at the end of his bed and saw the cat there, circling to settle in for a nap. Peace smiled.

"Did you find your way aboard the ship just to follow me?" he asked, scooping the creature up. It purred sleepily and rubbed its head against his cheek. Peace smiled and set it down, allowing it to curl up again on the blanket. He got up carefully, dressed, and left the tent so as not to disturb it. He blinked in the early morning sun and started wandering around the camp. His dream preoccupied his mind.

Eventually he found his brother and together they roamed the tents.

They talked and laughed and discussed old days when they were younger. They talked for a very long time until evening started to set in. The wind began to pick up around them and dark clouds began to saturate the sky.

Justice looked up and grunted rather passively. "Bad weather," he said. "It looks like a thunderstorm will be upon us tonight."

"Funny how it seems to mirror our present state," said Peace. "The foreboding future looming before us."

"Aye," said Justice. "I wonder what it will bring."

Then suddenly, almost as if in answer to his question, there came the distant sound of flapping, of a dragon's wings beating. Justice's hand immediately went to his sword and Peace scanned the skies. From behind the enemy fortress's central peak, the form of Ember slowly rose up into the evening air, a man upon his back.

Deception.

They rose until they were well above the towers and stayed there hovering in the sight of all. Then slowly, Ember turned and flew off into the distance, his silhouette growing smaller and smaller until it settled on a mountain peak several miles behind the city. Then all was silent except for the howling wind.

Peace turned to look at his brother. "What do you suppose that was for?"

Justice grunted and turned back toward the camp. "He wants us to follow him, possibly leaving our army behind."

Peace turned and tried to keep pace alongside his brother. "So, will we go? Will we try to find them?"

Justice grunted. "I will certainly find them, but not now. First, we handle their men, and then we will hunt them down."

Peace was silent for a moment, thinking about his dream. Then he spoke. "I think I know what I have to do."

"What do you mean?"

"I need to fight Deception alone. I had a dream, and in it Ember asked me to fight for him."

Justice rolled his eyes. "And did your dream tell you the outcome of that battle?"

"Well...no, it did not."

Justice turned to him, his eyes beseeching. "Peace," he said. "The dragon you once knew is gone. There is nothing left. If you try to reclaim him again, you will only be killed. That dragon has to die."

"If that is what slaying Deception means, that is what I will do."

"So you are willing to kill your dragon?"

"If that is what it takes to save him from Deception's grasp, then yes."

Justice looked him in the eye, pleadingly. "Then please, let us do it together. I didn't get to you in time before; don't let me make that mistake again."

Peace was silent. Justice placed his hand upon his shoulder. "Peace, when people talk about me, they say that I have no weakness, that I've given my heart to nothing that can be taken. But that's not true; I realized it the day you were almost stolen from me in the tower—I love you, my brother. I've lost so many people; please don't let me lose you too."

Peace looked at him and nodded.

"I understand."

"Good," said Justice. "Then let's end this together."

The evening grew later, and night fell. The camp slept, and in the distance thunder rumbled. Justice slept soundly for the first time in many nights; he did not feel the shadow that moved across him. In the distance, lighting flashed again but he still did not sense the form of his brother next to him, carefully placing something beside his bed.

"I'm sorry," the figure said. "But this is my path, my burden. Ember is my dragon, and it is his Rider alone that must decide his fate. I'm sorry."

The figure backed up, and then moved toward the tent flaps. A flash of lightning briefly illuminated his shadow and then he was gone.

* * *

Before the walls of the castle, a general stood with his army of two thousand behind him. Carefully he watched the cloaked figure on horseback ride off toward the mountain behind them. He grunted. He had been told that a man would pass by riding that way—his orders had been to let him through. Afterward, they were to start the attack.

He nodded and turned forward, leading his men in a march.

* * *

Determination burst into Justice's tent, waking the general abruptly.

"Sire!" he called. "Peace is gone!"

Justice leapt up from his bed, grabbing his sword. "What? Where!" he cried.

"Toward the mountain, sire. One of the guards saw him go but did not know to stop him."

Justice looked around wildly, then spotted something on the ground. Hesitantly, he reached out and picked it up. It was a Link, Ember's Link; the one Peace had always carried with him through all the battles and trials he had faced.

"What is he going to do?" asked Determination.

Justice stared at the Link; his mouth gone dry.

"He's going to kill Ember."

* * *

Peace rode as hard as he could. In the sky above him thunder crashed and lightning blazed, illuminating the dense blanket of clouds that smothered the sky. He rode on. Up ahead, he could see the mountain; it was smaller than it had seemed, but still very large. He could see a trail that led up its slope, a smooth, well-traveled path that wound its way up to the very top. Peace put his head forward as his horse charged up the trail.

"I'm coming Ember," he whispered. "I'm coming for you, my Eldar."

* * *

Justice strode out of his tent, his weapons strapped to his side.

"You can't go out there!" cried Determination, running to keep pace with him. "There's an army approaching, nearly two thousand strong! We'll never get past them!"

Justice stopped and looked out toward the ranks of men, slowly advancing toward them in the distance. He fumed, his face set as hard as stone and his eye alive with fury.

"We don't have time for this," he growled.

"Shall I summon our men to—"

"No!" roared Justice, his gaze locked on the approaching army. He began to march toward them with wide, powerful strides.

"I will deal with this alone."

* * *

Peace had nearly reached the end of the path. Above him he could sense the top of the mountain drawing near, the place where Ember was, where Deception would be. He grunted and spurred his horse up the final bend, rounded a corner, and suddenly found himself looking upon a wide plateau, the same one that had haunted his dreams. At the far side he saw Ember, tall, proud, and as magnificent as any dragon. In the center, between the two of them, was Deception. He was kneeling on the dusty ground, his saber drawn and its point stabbed into the dirt. Lightning illuminated his expression as he looked up.

Slowly, with a smile on his face, Deception whispered the words of an ancient verse: "Storm clouds gather, oceans rise, and judgment rains down from the skies; thunder rumbles in the darkened heights, beware the place that lightning strikes."

Peace slowly dismounted his horse, threw off his cloak, and drew his sword.

Deception rose and spoke again. "Three times has lightning struck. The first was at Watergate where the Dragon Rider Pact was shaken; the second was at World's End where it was broken; the third was on the shores of the Shadowlands where its hope was lost; and now the final time shall be here, where the Pact shall be destroyed forever."

Peace slowly approached the man, his sword held at the ready. "This battle is between us," he said. "If you think Ember is yours, then fight me for him. If you think that you deserve the name of Rider, then challenge me for it!"

Deception looked at him curiously; his eyes seemed to consider the request. "I have no reason to fight you," he said. "I could have Ember disarm you and bring you straight to me; why should I give up my advantage and fight a duel?" He swung his sword around in a circle, cocking his head to the side. "On the other hand, when all this is over and tales are told of this occasion, I think that I should like to be remembered as the one who fought and defeated the Dragon Rider."

He looked at Peace and smiled. "I accept."

* * *

The general held up his hand to stop the advance of his men. Out of the darkness before them a lone figure approached. His steps were resolute, his stride unfaltering. Thunder crashed in the sky above and a flash of lightning lit up the figure's face.

Justice.

The general drew his sword, fear running through him. What could make this man walk so deliberately, so at ease toward them? Did he fear nothing? He raised his weapon as the phantom figure neared until it stood before him—its sword undrawn, its cape billowing in the wind.

The figure spoke, "Good evening, general." Its voice was cold, unshaken.

The general shivered.

"What brings you and these men out here before me?" it asked. Then it cocked its head. "On second thought, I'm going to give you the benefit of the doubt and assume that your impressive display of arms is merely a salute of respect. Supposing for a minute, however, that you were here to oppose me, might I ask what your plan would be? To overcome me with pure numbers?"

The general gulped, fear racing through him. "I admit that I have seen large forces play decisive roles in battles," he said.

The figure laughed. "Decisive roles? Ha! Tell me, fine general, how many men did Ruthless take to oppose my fighting force of two hundred?"

"Nearly a thousand," said the general.

"And tell me, would you have considered Ruthless to be a lesser or greater commander than yourself?"

"Greater, by far," said the general. He couldn't keep his voice from shaking.

The figure made a firm stance, his feet planted on the ground. "Then listen well! Ruthless lies dead on the shore surrounded by three hundred of his finest men; I outwitted him! His entire force could not succeed in killing even one hundred of my men, and now his ship is under my control! Now I stand before you—and you think I fear your numbers? You think I fear weapons? I defended a city from Deception and all his dragons, I have overcome your greatest warrior, I fear nothing!"

The figure leaned in closer, examining the general's face. "But even if you do not fear me, there is one still greater, one whom I watched cast dragons out of the sky and who defeated six kingdoms besides. That man is the King, and he is coming. He told me himself; he will come with his armies, and upon his great dragon he will ride forth laying waste to every town, every stronghold, every kingdom in this whole land! You may think that you can stand against me but tell me how you can possibly hope to stand against him! His rage will be unstoppable, unbeatable; no one will survive his conquest!"

The figured stopped and cocked his head at the terrified, shaking general. "But you have not yet shown yourself to be my enemy. Yes, you have brought out a great force as though to provoke me, but you have not pitted yourself against the crown. The coming storm may yet pass you by; if you show yourself to be my friend, you will still be allowed to live here in your own land."

The general was shaking uncontrollably. So long had they lived under the terror of Deception, so long had they feared for their lives, so long had they lived in despair. He looked up trembling toward the calm figure. It placed a hand on its sword.

"But if you do not join me, if you prove yourself to be my enemy, then listen well: my name is Justice, and my father is the King!" He drew his sword halfway and lighting flashed against its steel. "What shall we call you?"

The general cried out and thrust his sword into the ground. The men behind him did the same. "Call us friends! I surrender; we all do! Make us a part of your kingdom, I beg you!"

The figure smiled and slid his sword back into its sheath. "Then I find you innocent of crimes against the crown, and on the King's behalf I accept you into our nation."

"Please," begged the general. "Please do not make us fight Deception; do not let us face his wrath!"

The figure smiled wider.

"Lend me your fastest horse, and I will see to it that you never do."

*  *  *

Peace and Deception circled on the darkened mountaintop. All around them the blackened sky rumbled and growled with waves of thunder that crashed in the distance. Lightning flickered over the ground, illuminating them. Peace waited until Deception twirled his sword around before making a sudden strike. Deception blocked the blow easily and smiled.

"I'll have to give it to you, you are determined," he said.

Peace cried out and charged his opponent, swinging and hacking his enemy's blade. Deception skillfully deflected the blows and then struck out himself, causing Peace to jump back.

"I wonder what your new name would have been?" Deception said, lunging again. "Persistence? Redeemer? How about Murderer?" He swung hard and again Peace had to leap back. Deception shook his head at him disapprovingly. "What are you hoping to accomplish? You know that my Curse entwines Ember's soul, that killing me will kill him."

"I do," Peace heaved and swung his sword, feeling its reverberations as Deception blocked.

"Then why are you doing this? I thought you loved him." He struck out again. "Have you become just as heartless as your brother?"

Peace ducked. "I want what is best for him; I'm here to set him free."

Deception laughed and suddenly attacked wildly, forcing Peace back as he desperately tried to block each blow. "Set him free? By killing him?" Deception shouted, keeping after his opponent. "Shouldn't Ember have a say in that? Who made you the one who decides the fate of his very life? What gives you the right?" He swung hard and Peace blocked, pushing back against its force.

"I'm his Rider; I've always had the right." He swung and Deception had to leap back.

"You are not his Rider!" Deception cried. "It's not your choice to make!" he kept after Peace with increasing speed and ferocity.

"Ember gave the choice to me," gasped Peace, desperately trying to defend himself from the hacking blade. "He gave it to me the day we swore our loyalty to each other. He said that he would let himself be led by his Rider, that he would trust me to do what was right."

"You are not his Rider!" screamed Deception, swinging his blade around in a blinding half circle and knocking the sword clear out of his opponent's hand. Peace stared at him in shock and slowly sank to the ground, defeated. He waited for Deception to stab him through the heart. Instead, Deception took a step back and smiled. He gestured toward Peace's fallen weapon with his saber.

"Again," he said.

* * *

Justice rode hard and fast, spurring his horse on to greater and greater speeds. He had to get there in time; perhaps he was already too late! He growled. No! This time he would make it. This time he would be there. He locked his eyes on the approaching mountain as lightning flashed ahead.

"Hold on, Peace, I'm coming for you."

* * *

Peace seethed, stood, and retrieved his fallen sword. Deception stood at the ready again.

Then Peace roared and charged, battling fiercely. Deception kept pace with him, blocking each blow as if he had rehearsed it all. "Why do you keep fighting? Do you think your dragon still cares for you? He chose me!"

Peace grunted, trying desperately to break through Deception's defenses. "You cursed him! He didn't have a choice."

Deception laughed. "Yes, I did curse him, but not at the beginning. He never could've lured you into my trap at World's End had he not had the freedom to contact you."

He swung his sword around, blocking Peace's blade, and then began to advance, swinging more and more wildly. "When I found him, he was in pain from your words at Watergate. He hated you! I simply talked to him, I laid my hand on him gently, and he turned to me. He always had the choice to resist, and he chose me!" He hacked harder and Peace gasped trying to defend himself.

"You lie! He would never forget me! He did not leave me!"

"He did!" cried Deception, glee in his eyes. "He left you! You hurt him so badly that he chose to live under my care out of *hunger*."

He advanced like a hunter going in for the kill. "This is your fault! You gave him up! He is *Mine*!" He swung his sword again and for the second time Peace's blade flew from his hand. Deception looked at his opponent, hate building in his eyes. Peace stared back at him, fear and despair clouding his. He looked to his sword and then back at Deception. The man appeared to be thinking.

"Go ahead. One more time."

Peace reached for his sword and Deception instantly lashed out and knocked it from his hand. "For years I was hunted by the King," he sneered. "How does it feel to be at another's mercy?" He eyed Peace's sword.

"Pick it up!"

Peace did so and the moment he lifted the point, Deception charged him, slashing in the angriest, wildest, and most hate-filled strokes he could. "How does it feel *Rider*, to be denied your dragon? How does it feel *Rider*, to have that which you long for be kept from you? How does it feel *Rider*, to look into the eyes of the creature you love most and have it loathe you? Hate you?"

Peace stumbled beneath his blows and nearly fell. He dove to the side and Deception kept after him. "For ten years I lived in the King's palace! For ten years I watched as the dragon that was rightfully mine was given, cherished, cared for by another! For ten years I watched my birthright flee from me and into the arms of your father. For ten years I lived in agony!"

"Glory was never your birthright," gasped Peace. He couldn't hold out much longer against Deception's fury. "You had no rights except what you had been given! You scorned the kindness my grandfather bestowed upon you! You could've had so much more had you not sold yourself to hatred!"

"Hatred was what he forced upon me!" cried Deception. "And just to prove it, when I'm finished with you, I will go and challenge the King. I will kill him, and after I do, I will take his dragon, lead it out into the castle courtyard, and have it slaughtered! I will relish making her pay for every ounce of pain she caused me!"

He swung his sword with fury, and for the final time knocked Peace's blade out of his grip. He snarled, pointing his sword at his opponent. "It's time we finish this."

Peace sank to his knees in a daze. Off to the side, he saw Ember watching passively, as if it were all a rehearsed play he had seen one too many times.

Deception grinned, his chest heaving a little. "It's all right," he said. "This is a good way to die. It's better for us all anyway."

"I am sorry, Ember," said Peace quietly. "I have failed you."

"Failed him?" said Deception with surprise. He sank down and spoke smoothly. "Peace, you did not fail him. He is not under your control, but he is happy. Can't you see that? He has everything he wants; he experiences elation and joy. Would you really tear it all away from him? Can't you let him be? If you really loved him, wouldn't you let him go?"

Peace stared at the ground, his eyes hardening and his fist tightening. When he spoke, his words were firm and even.

"It is because I love him, that for his own sake I would rather see him dead than in the hands of the likes of you!"

With a cry, Peace dove sideways and seized his sword as Deception slashed downward in rage. Instantly Peace was on his feet and hacking away at his enemy's defenses with unearthly force, driving him back further and further as Deception desperately tried to counter the unexpected assault.

And then suddenly Deception found that he was standing at the edge of the plateau with nothing but empty space behind him. Frantically he tried to push Peace back, but his opponent had come alive with a supernatural power—a power driven to protect what he loved most.

With a cry Peace swung a downward stroke and Deception blocked it with the flat of his blade, using both hands against the impact. Peace bore down on him and Deception struggled to push back, to keep his footing.

"What are you trying to prove?" he shouted. "That you can beat me in a sword fight? You've stopped nothing! The Pact will still be destroyed!"

With a shout Peace shoved Deception backward with his sword, hurling the man headlong into open space.

Peace watched as Deception fell, tumbling, before hitting a ledge that protruded from the mountainside. He landed full on his back and for several seconds lay completely still. Then he shifted slightly, groaning.

"You fool!" he said faintly. "You stupid fool."

And then Peace whirled around and found himself staring straight into the fiery eyes of Ember.

* * *

Justice had reached the foot of the mountain. He found the beginning of the path and immediately started up. The top of the mountain seemed so high, so far away. But he refused to give up. His brother was up there; Deception hadn't flown off. There had to be time. Justice desperately spurred his horse faster and faster up the treacherous incline. He had to make it.

* * *

Deception sluggishly and painfully struggled to his feet. He had survived the fall—even he was surprised by that. He could've died; had the fall been much further it would've killed him! He shook his head and carefully tried to get his footing, moving slowly and leaning on the rock wall for support. He spotted his saber on the ground and picked it up. His head pounded.

He started up the mountain path, limping painfully; it wouldn't be too far from this point by foot. He touched the Link around his neck. Through the Curse's shadow he couldn't gain a very clear impression of what was happening to Ember, but he had given the command to attack and knew well enough what was going on. Of course, he could've had the dragon come down and pick him up, but perhaps it was better this way. To have the dragon kill its own Rider. He smiled, though painfully. Thunder rumbled above him. It hadn't been his plan, but there was a sort of justice to it. It would do.

* * *

Peace dove to the side as the gigantic beast leapt for him. He landed in a roll on the dust, and it occurred to him that he had dropped his sword. He spun and saw it there by the edge, between the dragon's feet. Ember didn't notice though; he turned, growling with rage and leapt again.

Any other man would've died in those next few minutes. But Peace was still wearing his Link, and the years he had spent with Ember had taught him just enough about the way his dragon moved, how he attacked, that he was able to barely leap out of the way each time. Ember grew more angry by the moment and began to strike wilder and faster. He growled, he roared, he blasted the rocks with fire trying to hit his nimbler opponent, but Peace sensed each attempt in time to narrowly escape.

Lightning flashed across the sky and lit up his sword. He noted where it lay and tried to edge that direction. The next time Ember swiped at him, he ducked and dove in a manner that brought him closer to his weapon. Each time he felt that fire was about to strike, he leapt to the side and started moving as soon as he could get to his feet again.

Peace edged closer and closer, and the next time lightning flashed he saw his sword lying only a few feet away. He was almost there! Quickly, he turned around and ran for it; behind him, Ember growled a cry of rage that almost matched the thunder above. He took a blind swipe in the dark at the charging figure and hit him, sending his former Rider tumbling across the rocks.

Peace picked himself up and spotted his sword. Ember stood before him, crouched and ready to spring. It would have been wise for the dragon to simply destroy him with flame from a distance, but it was clear from his eyes that Ember was too enraged to think of that.

Peace dove for his sword, rolling across the ground, and managed to get his fingers around the handle. Behind him, Ember pounced, leaping like a tiger, claws extended to crush his victim. Sensing the attack, Peace, in one smooth motion, spun around, rising up on one knee as he did so, and lifted his blade point up toward Ember's heart.

His eyes met Ember's. He watched the dragon in midair above him almost as if in slow motion. And in that one moment everything Ember was flashed before his eyes. He saw the hatchling he had raised, the little creature that had fled to him during thunderstorms, he saw the friend whom he had spent nearly his whole childhood with, the companion that had kept him company for three years in the wilderness, the comrade that had blasted its way out of a prison to rescue him and flown through tremendous pain to get him to safety, the dragon that he loved with all his heart, and Peace found that he could not do it. He could not kill Ember.

He lowered his sword.

With a crash that shook the earth Ember landed upon him, breaking his leg and sending his weapon spinning and bouncing over the cliff's edge. Peace cried out in great pain, staring up into the dragon's eyes, eyes that held no care, no compassion—only death. Peace felt them glaring at him as Ember raised his head up, fire forming in the back of his throat and lightning flashing fiercely behind him.

And then Peace saw it. Something that glimmered in the air above him, dangling from the dragon's neck. Time seemed to slow as Peace reached out, caught hold of it, and saw that it was a medallion. A vague memory formed in his head of Deception placing a chain around Ember's neck at World's End. He turned it so that it reflected the dim light and saw that it bore the design of two snakes twirling and entwining themselves around a small emerald in the center.

*...My Curse entwines Ember's soul...*

Peace shook his head, barely daring to believe. A barrage of words from the past assaulted him.

*...It is likely that Ember would not remember you...*

*...The dragon you once knew is gone. There is nothing left...*

*...Even if we could break the Curse, it would only leave him lost and alone...*

*...He is mine now—you have been entirely forgotten!*

Peace gritted his teeth.

*You lie.*

And he snapped the chain. The effect was immediate. Ember roared as though he had been stabbed and leapt backward off him. Peace felt the medallion in his hand which had been cool only a second before suddenly burn red-hot and glow orange. He cried out in pain but gripped it harder, smashing the accursed thing against the rocks to shatter it. The metal held firm. He looked up at Ember and saw him crouched a few feet away, crying out and jerking side to side as though possessed. Through his Link, Peace suddenly felt the fragments of a consciousness.

*Peace...Peace! Is that you?*

Peace let out a cry of joy. "You're here!" he shouted. "Ember! I knew you hadn't forgotten me!"

*There...there was always...a part of me that remembered.*

The dragon before him shook and shivered. Peace felt a war within his mind and watched as his eyes flickered from joy to rage.

*The...the...Curse. You have to...I can't—*

"Yes, you can," said Peace, wincing with pain as he rose to his good knee. "Come on; fight it off."

*I can't!* groaned Ember and he shook his head from side to side. *You...you have to destroy it...it's forcing me to kill you.*

"Here!" shouted Peace, flinging the Curse to the ground beside him. "Melt it! Destroy it with fire!"

*It won't let me! I don't have the power to do it. Take it and throw it over the side of the mountain. I'll be forced retrieve it, which will give you time to escape.*

"No," said Peace firmly, shaking his head. "I will not abandon you again to Deception's control."

*You have to...I'll kill you otherwise...I can't resist its hold much longer.*

Peace looked into his dragon's eyes, the old, noble eyes he had seen many times before. And suddenly, everything seemed clear.

"It's all right," he said calmly. "You can do it."

*Please! I can't...don't stay or I will hurt you!*

"I wanted to see you one more time before I died," said Peace clearly. "Now I am content. If you cannot fight against it, then I give you my permission, as your Rider, to kill me."

*No! Don't say that! I could not live with it...*

"It's ok. I forgave you already, for everything."

*But with you gone, what would become of me? I'd be lost; there would be no one to turn to.*

"It's all right; I've already taken care of it. What you need I cannot give you, but if you kill me now, I think you will be saved."

Ember looked directly at him, and for a moment, just for a moment, his eyes were purely those of an old friend.

*I can't bear to watch you die.*

"Then look away when you do it. I bear no ill will."

Ember tried one more time, his voice beseeching. *Please...Please don't...*

Peace held his gaze. His words were gentle and firm.

"Do it."

Ember shook his head and roared; the Curse began to overwhelm him again. He tried to regain control.

*I loved you; I would have given my life for you.*

"I know," said Peace sadly, removing his Link and tossing it to the ground beside him. "And I would do the same for you."

The dragon before him shook and tried to turn away but could not. Then it closed its eyes and slowly turned its head back toward him, mouth open to breathe fire.

Without taking his eyes off the dragon, Peace slowly reached out with his burned hand and picked up the Curse from the ground.

"Ever since you were born," he said quietly, "you were enslaved. First to me and then to Deception." He held the Curse out above his head so that it would catch the brunt of the fire. "Today I release you from both."

Somewhere above them, lightning flashed.

* * *

Deception rounded the final bend and was pleased that he had arrived in time to see the Rider's demise. He grinned maliciously as he saw the dragon rise above the kneeling man, fire forming in its throat. His eyes narrowed. What was that Peace held in his hand?

Suddenly he jolted forward, his mind scrambling for a counter command.

* * *

Justice had nearly reached the top when he heard the fire blast. It might have been instinct, or it might have been a sensation from Ember's Link which he carried with him, but suddenly he felt as if it were over.

Justice shook his head, not willing to believe it; but now his face turned grim, and he placed his hand on his katana as he rode. His ride became colder, angrier.

Somewhere above him, thunder rumbled.

* * *

Deception had been too late.

With a cry he ran for the place where Peace had knelt. Ember seemed distraught, as though he had suddenly woken up and found himself in a strange and hostile place. He spotted Deception and something seemed to register in his mind. He moved over the place where his former master lay and growled. Without a second thought, Deception pulled out his red horn and blew it hard, sending the dragon screeching and cowering to the edge of the cliff.

Deception approached the charred form of Peace. He kicked it angrily and snatched at the fist that clutched the Curse, prying it open. The medallion had melted into a pool of gray liquid metal that ran out through his fingers into a puddle on the ground. The only thing that remained was the emerald, safe and alone in the palm of his hand.

Deception threw his head back and roared. The last of the Curses had been destroyed! It had been his power, his control; now Ember could be taken by anyone! Peace had died, but he had died saving the dragon's soul.

Ember trembled at the cliff edge. He seemed to be consumed by fear, by pain, by guilt. Deception rose slowly and walked toward the cowering dragon, his hand held out.

"It's all right," he said. "I'm sorry for your loss, truly I am. But let me lay my hand on you and you will feel better. We've only got each other now; don't be afraid. Let me comfort you again." The dragon looked at him beseechingly, overwhelmed by sadness, and then rubbed his great head against Deception's hand.

"There you are; good boy, good boy," he said soothingly, stroking Ember's scales. Slowly Ember grew quiet, and then passive as the familiar hunger comforted him.

Deception smiled, but only faintly. The dragon was under his control again—temporarily, but under his control. But without the Curse, Ember wouldn't hear his thoughts.

Deception looked over to where Peace's Link lay unharmed beside the still body. He approached it and stood above the deceased prince.

"You thought you were the Rider; you clung to that title to your death." He leaned closer. "Well guess who the Rider is now?" He reached down to pick up the Link.

Suddenly, he heard a cry and looked up in time to see Justice charging toward him on a horse, his arm extended as if he had thrown something. Deception leapt back as a dagger went sailing by him and clattered across the rocks. For a moment he looked back at the Link lying unprotected on the ground, but fear overcame him and instead he ran toward Ember with the pounding sound of horse hooves thundering behind. As quickly as he could, he mounted the dragon, turned it toward the cliff edge, and rode forward. Behind, Justice cried out and hurled his katana as they took flight. But Ember turned at the last moment and the sword bounced harmlessly off the scales of his left thigh.

Justice watched, helpless and shaking with rage as the two of them flew off into the distance. As they disappeared he slowly turned to the dead form of his brother whom he had been too late to save. And for the first time since he was a child, Justice wept.

In the darkened sky above him, rain began to fall.

* * *

"Take our men and anyone else who wants to come and set sail for Highland."

Determination nodded grimly. "Of course, sire."

"When you go," said Justice, "make a stop at the city of Hope, and take any left there who still wish to see the country they waited so long for."

"Yes, sire."

"Is something wrong?"

"Well, it's just...won't you be coming with us?"

Justice turned to look up at the sky, now clear and blue. The morning was bright and cheery.

"I don't know. Wait for three hours, and if I come back then I will sail with you. If I do not, then set out without me."

Determination nodded. "Understood, sire."

Justice turned to leave, but as he did so he looked briefly at the ship being loaded up for the journey home. Ruthless had been defeated, Deception was far away, and the Curse had been broken. In many ways, they had won. But it didn't feel that way.

He sighed and continued moving forward. At the gangplank, he noticed a cat pawing the ground and looking around as if it had lost someone. Justice turned away, mounted his horse, and rode for the mountain.

He arrived at the summit in under an hour. He dismounted, and for the next hour he carefully buried what was left of his brother. When he finished, the sun was well on its way to its peak in the sky.

He sat down heavily and looked at the mound of dirt where the Dragon Rider lay. Sadness overcame him. He remembered the day when Ember had been born, when his brother had brought the little hatchling over to the fire to name it. All the people and nobles there had been so happy—if only they had known! How would they have reacted if they had known that the creature Peace cuddled close to him would one day turn to destroy him? How hard would they have mourned if they knew that the thing he sheltered would grow up to kill him—that there was born that day the means of his death?

Justice looked down at his hand, which held the sealed envelope Peace had insisted he take. Now, alone on the mountaintop, he carefully broke the seal and opened the envelope. He read the letter inside with silence.

*My dear brother Justice,*

*I said not to open this unless I had been killed or captured. Knowing you, however, I assume that if I had been captured, you would be putting your time and energy into finding me rather than reading this. Therefore, I think I can suppose that either I have died, or will die shortly, and that Deception and Ember will have no doubt played a role in my death.*

*Deception's desire was to break the Dragon Rider Pact, but of course we both know that he has only halfway succeeded. As long as Ember remains alive the Pact survives, and I as his former Rider have the authority to choose who his next master will be. Having already discussed it with our father before I left, I have decided to hand the responsibility and the burden of the title over to you.*

*I know that you are bent on killing Ember, and since he will likely have been involved with my death, I can only imagine that resolution will have grown stronger. Therefore, I do not plead with you to spare his life, which I know would be fruitless.*

*Instead, I ask only that you save his soul, that you rescue him from the clutches of Deception and return home with him. Then you may, as the custom dictates, do to your dragon as you please; I give him to you. I only ask, as my dying request, that you try to save him from the lies that ensnare him and that if he is to die, then let him do so in his sound mind and in his rightful place: at your side.*

*If you accept this responsibility, then take up my Link and find my old friend; I know that if there is one person who has the ability to do so, it would be you. Return with him to the presence of the King and you will be named the next in line for the throne. You are the Dragon Rider now.*

*Godspeed, my brother.*

*Peace.*

Justice folded the letter carefully and placed it in his saddle bag. He looked one last time over the place where his brother lay, and then knelt down and picked up the Link from where it had been on the ground since the previous night.

"As you have requested, so will I do, my brother."

Then he stood up and walked to the place where his dagger had fallen the night before and picked it up. Next he found his katana and sheathed that as well. He mounted his horse and turned to face the north where Ember had flown. There was no sign of him now, but still Justice faced that direction, murmuring words under his breath.

"I'm coming for you Deception. You have killed my brother, taken his dragon, and attacked our homeland—now I come for you. While Peace remained, you could have begged for mercy, but now I make you a promise that you will face the full punishment of your crimes; you will not escape what you have done!"

His voice began to rise. "Flee from me if you can! Run as far as you are able, but I will overtake you! Hide yourself in the deepest of caves, but I will find you! Bar yourself in your strongest cities and bring forth your strongest armies, but I will overcome you! My name is Justice, and this day your life is demanded of you. There is no place, either in this land or any other, where you can escape me."

He lowered his voice and growled.

"I come, Deception—I come for you."


End of Book Two